AN AVALON CAREER ROMANCE

EMERALD SKY

Gerry O'Hara

Kathleen Flaherty doesn't know what to expect when she accepts a position at Shea Crystal in Ireland. A talented advertising copywriter, she seems to hit a stone wall with Connor O'Shea, the head of the glassworks.

The handsome, Stanford educated boss, doesn't want an American intruding on his traditional Irish company. But Kathleen is determined to prove herself and not allow his gruff remarks to lessen her confidence.

Much as she would like to dislike her boss and keep up a strictly professional relationship with him, she can't help but feel the chemistry that sparks between them. Slowly, she notices his warmth, intelligence and the little things that reveal how much he truly cares for her. Can she prove to Connor that she is capable of producing a successful marketing brochure and worthy of not only his trust but his love?

EMERALD SKY

•

Gerry O'Hara

Library of Congress Catalog Card Number: 00-110062
ISBN 0-8034-9463-7

Published by Thomas Bouregy & Co., Inc.
160 Madison Avenue, New York, NY 10016

PRINTED IN THE UNITED STATES OF AMERICA
ON ACID-FREE PAPER
BY HADDON CRAFTSMEN, BLOOMSBURG, PENNSYLVANIA

Dedicated to my family, with love always,
and to the Walshes of County Mayo, with fond memories.

Chapter One

Sitting at a table on the deck of a cafe on Fisherman's Wharf, Kathleen Flaherty toyed with the straw in her iced tea and scanned the entrance for John Forbes, her ex-boss. She was nervous about this meeting, sensing that the outcome would change her life dramatically and possibly irrevocably.

Until recently she had been an advertising copywriter with Harris and Forbes. She had been in line for a promotion that would have put her in the number two spot in her department, but John Forbes' sudden decision to sell the company had put her career on hold. Forbes had cited a heart condition as a major factor, but rumor had it that a decline in profits had swung the pendulum toward retirement.

The new corporation had its own staff, and like so many other takeovers, planned a clean sweep so they could run the company "their way."

Kathleen saw the writing on the wall and began sending out resumes. It had been a prudent move; she was notified by the new Chief Executive Officer that her services were no longer needed, and given two weeks pay and a letter of recommendation.

John Forbes had championed Kathleen's rise through company ranks and had not concealed the fact that he was grooming her to head the advertising department. Although she had tried to conceal her disappointment at seeing the goal thwarted by the buyout, Forbes was not insensitive to her plight. Still looking out for his protege, he had arranged an impromptu interview for a job with an Irish glassworks.

She was intrigued by the idea of going to Ireland; her parents were from County Mayo. Forbes had assured her that if she were willing to relocate for a short time, it would provide the additional reference necessary to step up in the field.

Although she loved San Francisco, nothing tied her to the city. Her parents were dead, she had no other relatives, and her only romantic involvement since college had been with a sales rep at Harris and Forbes, and that had ended on a strange note.

She had dated Brian Thomas, the company's golden boy—a whiz at marketing fine china. Brian had dazzled everyone with an idea to acquire a company that produced silverplated tableware. He had convinced Forbes that a coordinated dinnerware package would be attractive to the consumer and would stimulate sales.

Kathleen suspected that John Forbes had stretched himself too thin with this project and rumors began skating through the office that the company would fold without an infusion of new money.

Before the dust had settled from an announced takeover, Brian had cleaned off his desk and was out the door. No one had heard from him since. Kathleen fielded questions about Brian's disappearance with a standard "I don't know any more than you do." Although the answer was as dissatisfying to the questioner as it was to her, it was true.

"Kathleen!" John Forbes interrupted her reverie, greeting her warmly before sitting down.

Kathleen studied the sixtyish man sitting across from her. A man she regarded with respect and affection. He seemed to have aged since she last saw him. There were tell-tale lines around his mouth and eyes. It was obvious that he was a tired, if not defeated, man.

Not one to mince words, he immediately launched into the reason for their meeting.

"I'm glad you decided to interview for the position with Shea Crystal. I've known Theresa and Connor O'Shea for years. Their crystal factory is first rate. Theresa is eager to have an American help them develop a catalog to approach the American market. I'm convinced the job is yours if you want it.

"Six weeks in another country will be an adventure. And having total responsibility for a catalog will look good on future resumes. You will be able to write your own ticket when you return."

"John, I know you don't like to talk about it, but I have to know . . . was Brian in any way responsible for your decision to sell the company?"

"Let's just say that when Brian's plan fell through, any hope for boosting profits were gone. Times are bad. The corporation that purchased Harris and Forbes can take a write-off if they lose money on one of their subsidiaries. All a write-off gave me was indigestion. It meant less money in everyone's paycheck, including mine.

"It's better this way. It was time for me to retire. I only wish it didn't mean dashing your plans."

"I sent resumes to a dozen companies. I didn't get to the interview stage with a single one. I wondered if there was speculation about Brian and if my association with him made the rounds of the rumor mills."

"Brian made mistakes. We all make mistakes. Unfortunately, his were costly. And he has a difficult time admitting to failure. That's probably why he left so quickly. Not very courageous, but human."

"You're very forgiving, John."

"Anger doesn't help. I know that you and Brian were tight for a while, and you are probably hurt by his unexplained move. The best advice I can give you is to forget him.

"Even if you have been linked to Brian's fiasco, my recommendation will carry more weight than gossip. And your experience . . . the copy on the fall catalog alone, will put you in good stead for this job."

"I hope you're right."

The hostess ushered an attractive, stylishly dressed woman to their table and John quickly rose to greet her. His Cheshire cat expression as he embraced the woman indicated that she was from the glassworks. She appeared to be in her late 30s. She wore her glossy black hair in a smooth chignon that accented an alabaster complexion.

"Theresa, I'd like you to meet Kathleen Flaherty, the advertising person I told you about."

"I'm so glad to meet you, Kathleen. John had wonderful things to say about your association with his company. He showed me a sampling of your work; the catalog is impressive. I'm eager to discuss the position we need to fill. I had hoped my brother would meet us, but he seems to have been delayed."

"Would you like a glass of wine, Theresa?" John

asked as the waiter hovered. "A chardonnay, perhaps?"

Theresa nodded absently. It was obvious that she wished to get to the point.

"We have an established glassworks, Kathleen, but our trade has been limited to our own country and Great Britain. We plan to enter the American market in the fall and by this time next year, I hope every household in the United States will be acquainted with our glass."

"That's an ambitious goal."

"But not unattainable. A sharp advertising person and a complementary line of china could provide an advantage. Since John has already given us a lead in one direction, I'm hoping the other will also be accomplished before we leave San Francisco."

"I told Theresa you were considering a change of scene," Forbes prompted, "and that this opportunity might be suitable for both of you."

"It's been ten years since my brother attended Stanford University," Theresa said. "A decade since Shea Crystal has had any input from this side of the Atlantic. I am convinced that an American advertising person would provide the insight that we are lacking.

"John tells me that you've had experience in graphic arts."

"I studied commercial art and broke into advertising by doing paste-up and layout."

"My brother and I are looking for a copy writer who can also handle artwork and layouts. It's a large undertaking; you would have to be willing to be a one-woman advertising department. It's only for the first catalog, though, and only a limited number of designs will be featured. It may sound overwhelming, but John assured me that you were the right person for the job."

"Have you done much interviewing for the position?" Kathleen asked.

"None. To be honest, my brother is fiercely loyal to our countrymen. He views hiring an outsider as tantamount to treason. It has taken all of my energies to try and convince him otherwise. You are the first person recommended to me since he agreed to consider outsiders.

"Besides, finding someone capable of producing first-rate copy and the ability—and willingness—to be responsible for artwork and layout as well, isn't easy. Perhaps impossible given our time frame. When John told me about you, it seemed the answer to a successful advertising scheme. Are you interested?"

"The job sounds challenging. And I've never hesitated to work long hours when necessary. John can attest to that."

Kathleen looked at her ex-boss and he nodded confirmation.

"My parents were from Ireland. I've always

hoped to someday visit the town where they grew up."

"Then you must accept." Theresa smiled. "We're prepared to cover your airfare and we'll more than meet your present salary plus a bonus when the catalog is completed."

"I can't believe this, it's happening so fast!" Kathleen said.

"I'll admit, John spoke so highly of you, that I had nearly made up my mind before meeting you. Now, I'm doubly sure about asking you to join our staff."

"It sounds like a marvelous opportunity, Kathleen," John Forbes said, "but if you think you need more time . . ."

"We're returning to Ireland in three days. I need an answer now so that I can proceed with airline reservations immediately.

"I wouldn't tie you to anything more than one catalog, then we can reassess whether or not you wish to stay on."

Advertising jobs weren't begging in the Bay Area, and maybe a change of scene would do her good. She hadn't admitted to anyone that Brian's disappearing act bothered her, but it did. She felt bruised by his dismissal. Losing job and boyfriend at the same time undermined her self-confidence. The job at Shea Crystal might be a prescription for renewed well-being.

But could she pack up and fly to another continent so easily?

"This is short notice."

"Nonsense! You don't have to worry about accommodations, you will be a guest in our home.

"Our estate is on Achill Island," Theresa pronounced the "ch" as "k." Her smile widened, and she touched Kathleen's hand. "Ireland is so small you can drive from one shore to the other in a matter of hours. It would be easy enough for you to visit your family's hometown while staying with us."

"You've thought of everything. How can I refuse?"

"Wonderful!" Theresa clasped Kathleen's hand.

"I'm sorry I'm late," a husky voice interrupted.

The newcomer was built like a soccer player. His jacket hugged a broad chest and wide shoulders and slimmed to accent trim hips. He exuded raw strength tempered by an almost regal posture. His square jaw had a cleft that hinted at humor, but was contradicted by an intense expression in his amber eyes. His bronze hair was a thick, coarse mass of waves that ended in curled tufts at the collar.

He pulled out a chair and sat down. A smile tugged at the corners of his mouth, lighting his face with a handsomeness that appeared chiseled by an artist. But this man was real, he was not made of stone or bronze, and when his gaze locked with Kathleen's, she felt a jolt.

"Good to see you again, John." He shook hands with Forbes, but his attention was riveted on Kathleen.

"Connor, I'd like you to meet Kathleen Flaherty," Forbes said.

"Hello, Kathleen Flaherty." His deep voice contained only a whisper of a brogue. His accent had obviously been mellowed by his years at Stanford.

"Hello, Connor." Kathleen thought there was something compelling about the stranger—something beyond the mere attraction of his good looks.

"So this is the advertising person you told us about, John. I don't know how much you know about our company, Kathleen, but we've been conducting interviews all week," Connor said. "We're looking for a top-notch advertising person to help us develop a new catalog."

"Connor . . ." Theresa tried to interrupt, but Connor had taken charge, and was not to be detoured.

"We still have a few other people to talk to, but you seem to be on the top of the list. After all, anyone John recommends will be given special consideration. Of course, we'll want to check your references, perhaps have you work up a sample layout . . ."

Theresa and John Forbes exchanged uncomfortable glances. How could they tell him she had already been hired without making him feel like a fool? Kathleen wondered.

"Uhh, Connor, Kathleen already has . . ." John Forbes was trying to get the conversation back on track, but Connor was not to be deterred.

"The position is one of extreme responsibility. It will take more than an eight-hour day to complete this catalog in time for the Christmas buying season. Would you be willing to dedicate that much time to a project?"

"Yes . . . of course . . ." Kathleen stammered. Wasn't anyone going to rescue her?

"Of course, if you are unable to relocate to our country immediately, we needn't discuss this any further."

Where was this conversation going? Connor seemed ready to dismiss her as a prospective employee when it was too late for that kind of talk. Kathleen glanced around frantically, eyes pleading for help. Theresa and John's expressions were fraught with dismay.

"I've already hired Kathleen," Theresa blurted.

Kathleen watched Connor's expression change as if a window shade had been drawn across his face, then quickly released. The newly arranged lines around his mouth and eyes no longer spoke of friendliness; they were almost hostile. His gaze narrowed and he stared at his sister in surprise.

"I'm afraid I got carried away by Kathleen's

qualifications and our need to seal an agreement as soon as possible. We are running out of time, Connor. It was a godsend when John recommended Kathleen. I was sure that you would be as pleased to have her on our staff as I am," Theresa added.

"Hiring an advertising person was supposed to be a joint decision, but since it's done, it's done. I'm not going to quibble."

Kathleen was uncomfortable with all this talk. It was obvious that Connor was not happy with his sister's move to hire her without his approval. He was decidedly unaccustomed to having his authority usurped. She hoped it wasn't going to cause problems later.

"You're quite fortunate, Connor. Kathleen's one of the best copywriters that ever worked for me. Her knowledge of advertising layout and graphics will be a definite bonus for Shea Crystal," John Forbes said.

"I have the utmost respect for your opinion, John." He turned to Kathleen.

"I'm taking you on faith, Kathleen. I had expected to have some input in hiring, so you can appreciate my reaction to the situation." A lock of hair fell across Connor's forehead and he impatiently brushed it aside with the back of his hand.

"I don't doubt John's testimonial, but finding the right person to design the catalog is a serious affair. I would hate to find out later that my sister hired you as a result of two women finding themselves simpatico."

Kathleen's mouth fell open, and her back stiffened at the remark. It wasn't her fault he'd made a fool of himself, acting like a charging bull, blind to anything but his target. Making himself sound so important, trying to impress her with a story about how many people were standing in line for the job! He deserved to have the wind knocked out of his sails.

"Entering the American trade is an important enterprise for us," Connor continued. "A rather large budget has been allocated for the catalog. We project a twenty percent increase in sales from the American market, so you can understand that creating an effective catalog is our top priority.

"Of course, I accept John's assessment of your ability, but this is a major undertaking. We can't be too careful. If the catalog fails, Shea Crystal follows suit. You will be working on a tough deadline, which means long hours and all of your concentration. I just ask that you think it through, and if you have any doubts, you should reconsider accepting the position."

"I'm sure John will back me up when I say that my reputation for following through on a project has never been questioned."

"That's true," John agreed. "Kathleen isn't afraid

of work, and her organizational skills are outstanding. You won't be sorry about this alliance."

"I would never question your appraisal of people or situations, John.

"I've got to be going. I postponed an important appointment for this interview . . . I mean, introduction. Let's have lunch tomorrow, John. I'd like to make up for cutting this meeting short."

The two men shook hands. Connor nodded to his sister. "Theresa, I'll see you back at the hotel. Miss Flaherty, I'll see you in Ireland. Have a good trip. Sorry if I seemed abrupt."

He stepped closer to Kathleen, his face only inches away from hers. She could breathe in the musky scent of his aftershave. He extended his hand and she took it. His grip was firm.

"Glad to have met you, Connor," she said, not quite sure that she meant it.

He smiled in acknowledgement of her words, but she sensed that it was only a gesture of courtesy. He was not reconciled to having her on the staff of Shea Crystal yet.

What was it going to be like to work with him? What had she gotten herself into? Instead of respite from personal chaos, was she stepping into a maelstrom?

Chapter Two

Kathleen lifted her suitcase and tote bag from the slow-moving conveyor belt. Beside her, a family of six struggled with five oversized pieces of luggage. The mother tended to the youngsters while the father crammed the suitcases onto a baggage carrier that resembled an ailing supermarket cart, its rusted wheels squealing as they splayed side to side.

Four stewardeses, dressed in Aer Lingus' blue and green, trailed a dolly stacked with overnight cases and garment bags. They quickened their steps to catch up with the men in the crew.

Shannon Airport was a marked contrast to the hubbub of San Francisco's air terminal. The Aer Lingus jet appeared to be the only plane disembarking passengers.

Passport ready, Kathleen walked through the customs line then joined the exodus to the lobby. She paused to look for Theresa while other passengers passed by. Some rushed from the lobby with relatives in tow or scurried to the car rental desks that banked one side of the building. A few unhurried vacationers ambled toward the Irish Tourist Board counter for last-minute advice on sightseeing.

Kathleen felt stranded in the midst of the other people's singlemindedness. While airborne, she'd had time to question the intelligence of accepting a job with Shea Crystal. As much as she needed employment, and looked forward to being in Ireland, working under Connor O'Shea's scrutiny would be difficult.

"Kathleen!"

Kathleen turned at the sound of her name and saw Theresa approaching. The smile on the other woman's face helped erase some of her doubts.

"I was worried that you might change your mind." Theresa gave Kathleen an enthusiastic hug. "I would have been devastated if you hadn't shown up."

Theresa took Kathleen's suitcase and they walked out of the terminal. Marshmallow clouds melted across an azure sky. The air was crisp and Kathleen buttoned her jacket to block the chill that tried to seep through her clothing.

"Welcome to Ireland, Kathleen. The sun is shining for your arrival; 'tis a good sign."

Theresa unlocked the tailgate of a gold Volvo station wagon and swung Kathleen's luggage inside.

As they drove, Kathleen concentrated on the scenery to take her mind off the unsettling experience of being on the left side of the road.

In Galway, brick rowhouses stood in straight lines like soldiers called to attention. Once past the city, the low profile of farmhouses set the tone. Cinder block was used extensively and as a result the houses had sharp angles and few soft, curving lines. Still, they were attractive and not unlike the ranch style prevalent in California from the '50s building boom.

They stopped at a railroad crossing and waited while a couple of freight cars and a caboose passed. When the clack of the wheels was just an echo, two women scurried from an adjacent bungalow and pulled the steel guard gate away from the tracks. They waved Theresa through and called "good day" to her.

Theresa smiled. "We aren't quite as automated as your country, but we manage."

It took nearly three hours to reach Achill Island. They drove across a concrete bridge and onto a road that cut through desolate terrain. In the distance, a mountain rose from the edge of the bay.

Rock walls separated pastures as well as neighbors as they meandered between a scattering of box-like gray, slate-roofed cottages. Sheep grazed the pastures with newborn lambs clinging to their sides.

A farmer, his face weathered from sun and age, walked along the other side of the road, prodding a small herd of slow-moving cows. His gray coat flapped against his legs in rhythm with his step, and a ragged black-and-silver border collie tagged along at his heels.

Theresa turned the Volvo onto a road hedged by bushes growing in wild abandon. The upper branches were so heavy they fell forward and meshed into a canopy, blocking the sunlight. When they emerged from the leafy tunnel Kathleen blinked at the sudden brightness. Her eyes refocused and the first thing that appeared, as though it were an apparition, was a Georgian home big enough to qualify as a mansion. It was a startling contrast to the spartan farmers' cottages they had passed, yet it did not look out of place.

"Land's End," Theresa announced. "Welcome to our home."

It took a moment before Kathleen realized that Theresa had spoken the name of her estate, not the end of the secluded road.

"I hadn't expected anything so impressive."

"It seems much too big since our parents died. Your company will be a pleasant addition."

They got out of the car, removed the luggage and walked to the house.

Clusters of crimson rhododendron and multicolored tulips vied for attention along a slate path. Thick clusters of Scotch broom flanked the sides of the house and created a gentle melding of the carefully tended front garden and the vigorously wild shrubbery spilling down the hillside to the sea. Half a dozen horses grazed in a nearby pasture.

They were met at the door by a middle-aged woman who might have been considered homely if it weren't for luminous green eyes that made her face sparkle.

"This is our housekeeper, Jennie Ryan." Theresa introduced the two women. Jennie's effusive greeeting suggested that she was as pleased to have company as her mistress.

"I'll take you upstairs while Jennie puts the teapot on."

They walked up a crescent-shaped staircase and Kathleen detected the lingering scent of lemon oil on the gleaming mahogany bannister.

Theresa halted outside a spacious bedroom that was papered with clusters of baby roses. "This will be your room."

The soft glow of pink evoked Kathleen's first sense of relaxation in days. A mahogany four-poster was framed by a ruffled, dusty-rose canopy that spilled folds of satin behind a carved headboard.

Beside the bed a Chippendale nightstand held a crystal vase filled with freshly cut lilac.

"I love it, Theresa, it's so warm and feminine."

Connor's sister flushed with pleasure. "This room has always been one of my favorites. I can remember Mother poring over the catalogs to choose the wallcovering and fabrics. It's been a long time since my parents died, but sometimes a pleasant memory makes me realize how empty the house is without them."

"I know how you feel." Kathleen touched her arm.

"I think it's more difficult for Connor," Theresa said. "He kept his grief locked inside until it became a driving force propelling him towards Father's dream of making our glassworks a top contender in the field. Sometimes I fear the fight to make Shea Crystal overtake Cavan and Galway will consume my brother. And yet, it's Connor's decision. I have no right to interfere. How I ramble . . . Jennie must have tea waiting for us."

"I'll wash up first," Kathleen said.

"Call me if you have trouble finding the kitchen," Theresa said before disappearing into the hall.

Kathleen walked to the window and looked out at the vast land surrounding the house. A short distance away, a huge stone building hugged the curve of the road. She did not have to be told that it was the glassworks.

Was Theresa's overbearing brother there now? Kathleen could not cast aside the anxiety of working for Connor O'Shea. They had gotten off to a bad start. She only hoped that he could put that behind him. She had to admit that she was guilty of a judgment call based on that one incident, too, and that wasn't quite fair. They both needed a second chance if they were going to work together. Still, she could not ignore the intuitive sense that he was a man of many moods. He would not be an easy man to work with even after she proved her competence in advertising.

Kathleen went downstairs and followed the aroma of freshly baked bread to the kitchen.

"Sit down," Theresa said, as Jennie placed a tray with tea and sandwiches on the round oak table. "A cup of tea will relax you before I give you a short tour of Shea Crystal."

"How long has your glassworks been in business?" Kathleen asked. "I'm familiar with Cavan, Waterford and Galway, but I had never heard Shea mentioned before I met you."

"We aren't as old as some of the other glass companies; originally, our family were farmers. In 1843, my great-great uncle, William Shea, left Achill Island for an apprenticeship at Waterford. He knew he risked losing his inheritance when he rejected farming, but he was an artistic man and tilling the soil didn't satisfy him.

"Eight years later, Waterford closed its doors and their furnaces were to remain cold for an entire century. William had become a master craftsman and when he returned to Land's End he convinced his father that a fortune could be made in producing quality crystal."

"That simple?"

"Of course not." Theresa laughed. "If I don't resist the urge to embellish we'll be here all day.

"Michael Shea wasn't opposed to his son's idea because the farm had ceased to be prosperous. William had learned more than the art of creating fine crystal during his years at Waterford. He had accumulated a working knowledge of managing a glass factory."

"I'm curious about the 'O' not being part of your family name when the glassworks came about."

"Ah, that. In the early years, the Sheas were prolific and to mark one family from another in the town, the 'O' was added to the succeeding generations. It indicated 'son of' the previous Sheas.

"Enough talk about my family. Let's go to the glassworks so you can see our crystal."

They left the house and walked along a narrow road edged by a low stone wall that continued past Kathleen's line of vision, interrupted only by further extensions running down the hillside.

Shea Crystal was built of quarried rock, but unlike Land's End, it had not been glazed with plaster.

The natural appearance of the exposed stone produced a look of raw strength. The factory was built like a fortress, with turrets that could well have been battlements, guarding the crest of the hill. Although impressive, the simplicity of the common stone made it seem like a skyward extension of the meadow fence. Shea Crystal did not impose upon the landscape, it was part of it.

Smoke rose like thick, dark clouds from a bank of chimneys, indicating that the glassblowers were at work. Kathleen and Theresa walked through a parking lot that was jammed with bicycles and compact cars.

The two women entered a small front office and Kathleen was introduced to the receptionist, Clare Kelly, who welcomed her in a thick brogue.

"I'll have to see if there are any messages before I show you the display room," Theresa said.

The well-oiled efficiency of Theresa's office was softened by an attractive set of watercolor paintings. Theresa picked up a note from her desk and her face became etched with frown lines.

"Trouble?" Kathleen asked.

"I missed an important call. My brother will be furious! I was supposed to arrange a meeting with someone he met in San Francisco who may be able to assist us in acquiring a line of china."

The door opened and a man in his mid-40s stomped into the office. "I'm glad you're back!

Connor has been roaring about the shipment for Burns and Sons. He claims they haven't made good on their last order and he wants to know why we should expedite this one."

"Because I gave my word," Theresa answered. "Burns is good for the money. There was a mixup over the terms of payment but I talked to him yesterday and he assured me we would receive a check by return mail."

"I hope you're right, luv, because Connor will have both our heads if you're wrong."

"Everything will be fine," Theresa assured him. "We have a new addition to our staff, Sean. Kathleen Flaherty will be in charge of developing the new catalog. Kathleen, this is Sean Murphy, our general foreman."

"Welcome, Kathleen." Sean extended his hand. "Theresa can use your help. I swear if she hadn't found someone to work on the catalog, Connor would have her doing it herself. And she already does everything else!"

"You're exaggerating, Sean," Theresa protested.

"Am I now? I don't think so, luv, but I haven't time to argue the point, I've got to get back to work. Nice meeting you, Kathleen."

After Sean left, Theresa spoke. "Sean has been with Shea Crystal for eight years; he was with Cavan before that. He is an excellent trouble shooter and Connor's right arm. I often wonder how we got along before he joined our staff."

"He's rather good looking," Kathleen said.

"Yes." Theresa quickly averted her eyes and nervously fidgeted with the collar of her dress, smoothing an imaginary wrinkle.

"Shall we go see the display? I'll tell Clare where we'll be." She spoke to the receptionist through an intercom, then said to Kathleen, "I'm anxious to see your reaction to our crystal."

They entered the display room. Overhead, like an ice-glazed waterfall sparkling in sunlight, crystal teardrops cascaded from a dozen chandeliers. Rainbows danced from prism to prism, like fluttering butterflies.

"We're proud of our work." Theresa's hand scribed an arc encompassing the room. "I hope someday Shea Crystal will be a household word in America."

"It certainly deserves recognition." Kathleen picked up a goblet and studied it. The design was etched deeply. A half starburst, its rays fanned outward toward the lip of the glass. It was quality lead crystal and Kathleen knew that if she twirled a dampened finger around the rim, the glass would sing with the purest melody.

The door opened and Connor burst into the room. "Clare told me I would find you here. Where were you all morning? The place is ready to fall apart."

"I drove to Shannon to pick up Kathleen."

"I see. Hello, Kathleen. I hope you had a pleasant flight."

"Yes. It was thoughtful of Theresa to pick me up herself."

"Truthfully, she should have sent one of the men to meet the plane. Our entire day's schedule has been turned upside down without her."

"Connor!" Theresa said sharply.

"I'm sorry to be an imposition," Kathleen said.

"Not at all," Theresa said.

"I guess I should have been here earlier to welcome you to Ireland, or at least to Shea Crystal, but I've been too busy for social niceties."

"I really hadn't considered a polite 'hello' such a heavy responsibility, Connor."

Connor looked startled by Kathleen's retort. Laugh lines crinkled around Theresa's eyes, but she kept a breaking smile under control. Kathleen knew that her smart remark did not gain points with Connor, but she was too tired from the overseas flight to care.

"I came to tell you both that there's a meeting at three o'clock. My office." That message delivered, Connor turned and strode to the door. Opening it, he hesitated a moment. "Oh, yes, please forgive my lapse in manners. May I welcome you to Shea Crystal, and to Ireland, Kathleen Flaherty." Then he was gone.

Kathleen balled her hands into tight fists, trying to control her irritation. Was the "welcome" sincere, or another temperamental pronouncement? His tone had been cordial enough; was her ambiguous reaction colored by their first encounter?

"I had hoped you could spend the remainder of the day recovering from jet lag. I didn't realize Connor had a meeting on the calendar."

A short time after they returned to Theresa's office, Clare brought a tea tray with cookies and biscuits.

"I feel as though I have inconvenienced you," Kathleen said. "Your brother made it obvious that I've taken you from some very important matters."

"On the contrary. Things rarely run smoothly at my end, and Connor is bound to complain. Still, he rarely interferes with my decisions. I think he believes I'm the only one who can handle this facet of the business. One thing is certain, I'm the only one who would put up with it."

Although Theresa smiled, Kathleen noticed worry lines tugging at her mouth and playing around her eyes.

Putting her teacup down, Theresa said, "We should get on to the meeting."

They walked upstairs to Connor's office. It was

large but sparsely furnished with masculinely proportioned oak pieces.

Sean Murphy stood by the window, fidgeting with the cord on the blinds. He turned, said a perfunctory hello to Kathleen and spoke to Theresa in irritation.

"Just like Connor, with his penchant for punctuality, to keep us waiting this time." Sean nodded toward the clock.

Before the minute hand edged straight up, the door opened and Connor entered the room. Raced in, Kathleen thought as she heard the click that indicated it was exactly three o'clock.

"Shall we get started?"

Connor commanded rather than asked and Kathleen felt like snapping a military salute. He looked directly at her, his gaze boring into her with an intensity that made her skin tingle. Although there was arrogance in his look, Kathleen realized that was not what spurred her reaction. There was an indefinable sensuality to the way Connor assessed her. He took in every curve and angle of Kathleen's body in a quick but defiant study, then returned to her face. She could feel the warmth of a flush brushing her cheeks and cursed herself for showing that he bothered her.

"Did you bring a pad so you can take notes, Miss Flaherty?"

Of course she hadn't. She had no idea she would

be attending a meeting within hours after stepping off a transatlantic jet. His expression was smug. Did he take satisfaction in making her appear incompetent?

Theresa rescued her. "I'm going to share my notes with Kathleen."

Connor nodded to his sister. Then, as if he had gotten the unpleasantries out of the way so that he could proceed to more important matters, he began talking about the new project.

Connor exuded power and self-confidence. With good reason, Kathleen thought. She did not doubt that he would accomplish anything he set out to do. Right now, it wasn't his overbearing manner that came across, it was his infectious enthusiasm. Grudgingly, Kathleen began to respect Connor for his straightforward manner in outlining the steps necessary to corner a healthy portion of the American crystal market. With a nod in Kathleen's direction, he admitted that he expected the new catalog to play an important role in luring orders from the finest stores in America.

"It will have to be an outstanding catalog. We will be pumping a great deal of money into its production. We cannot settle for less than perfection! I want to see some innovative, copy that will make every buyer in the United States rush to carry a full line of Shea Crystal."

There was no malice in his voice. He honestly

expected her to be a superwoman in the advertising department. She hoped that she would meet his expectations.

The meeting lasted an hour. Kathleen was drained; she had begun her overseas flight the morning before and had not slept on the plane. Leaving Connor's office, Kathleen told Theresa she would have to call it a day.

"Unless you have something you want me to attend to right now, I'm going to walk back to the house. If I don't get a couple of hours rest I'll fall asleep at the dinner table."

"Kathleen, how thoughtless of me; you must be exhausted. I'll walk you home."

"You've taken enough time from your duties; I'll be fine."

They went downstairs together and before Kathleen left the factory, Theresa told her that dinner was at seven. Almost apologetically, she added, "Promptly. You know how Connor is about punctuality."

"I won't be late."

Walking towards Land's End, Kathleen studied the house. She hadn't noticed it before, but from this angle the mansion appeared intimidating; the big old Georgian was a bold, aggressive fortress that would resist the intrusion of outsiders. It was Connor's house and each straight line looked as unyielding as the man himself.

Chapter Three

The day had been interminably long—it seemed like weeks since Kathleen had slept. A headache hovered at the edge of her consciousness, threatening to intrude if she did not immediately make contact with a pillow.

Kicking off her shoes, she got into bed and pulled the down comforter up to her chin. It settled around the curves of her body, hugging and coaxing her into relaxation. She closed her eyes and was asleep within minutes.

Distant, muffled voices woke Kathleen. Disoriented, she raised herself to a sitting position. Remembrance: She was in Ireland. At Land's End. Connor O'Shea's home. And Connor had a penchant for punctuality. She threw off the comforter; she had overslept.

Dinner at seven! She had less than 15 minutes to freshen up; no time for a brisk shower that might infuse life into her tired body.

She went into the bathroom and splashed cold water over her face, then watched her day-old mascara make muddy tracks down her cheeks. How could there be even a trace left? she wondered, dabbing at the mess with a washcloth.

She fought a compulsive urge to scurry downstairs without regard to her appearance, and changed into a silky blue long-sleeved blouse with a wide bow at the collar. The long hours spent in a high-backed airplane seat had crushed her hair. She quickly brushed the soft waves and fluffed it with her fingers, trying to coax a semblance of body into the limp mass.

If only she hadn't overslept! She glanced at her watch. She dare not be even five minutes late.

Take it easy, she told herself. She could not allow this man to tie her into knots. Soon Connor would become acquainted with her work and would have no cause to question her competence. Once he accepted her as a skilled professional, they would be able to strike a truce.

With that pep talk providing bravado, Kathleen hurried downstairs and entered the dining room. She breathed a sigh of relief; she was a few minutes early after all her rushing. Time to catch her breath and steady her nerves before encountering Connor again.

The room, with its herringbone wallpaper, projected an ambiance of southern gentility. The dark mahogany furnishings made Kathleen think of Tara in *Gone With The Wind.*

"Good evening, Kathleen." Connor's voice was deep and warm.

"Good evening, Connor. I was admiring this room, it's lovely." She knew the words sounded trite but they were safe, free of controversy and she was pleased that her voice sounded normal and did not give away the fact that her emotions were wreaking havoc on her.

A brisk "thank you" was his only acknowledgement of the compliment. He motioned for her to take the chair to his left as he took his place at the head of the table.

Theresa joined them. "Did you rest, Kathleen?" There was concern in her voice. "I feel terrible about putting you through a full schedule on your first day."

"It's all right."

Jennie served the first course and Kathleen suddenly realized how hungry she was. The soup, a delicious asparagus cream, was followed by broiled salmon that Theresa told her had been caught in nearby Clew Bay.

Although the atmosphere was mellowed by the fine food and wine, Kathleen could not shake the feeling that she was an intruder. It was awkward being the guest of an employer who obviously was not pleased to have her in his employ.

"Where were your parents from?" Connor asked. His amber eyes contained a golden luster. Kathleen was surprised by the sudden turn toward friendliness.

"Crossmolina," she answered.

"A lovely town," Theresa said. "One of County Mayo's finest young ladies' schools, Gortner Abbey, is located there."

"My mother attended Gortner Abbey. Grandfather was a constable and Mother was born in an apartment above the barracks in Crossmolina. I'm anxious to visit the town and perhaps talk to people who knew our family."

"We have a friend who runs a bed and breakfast just outside of town; a lovely place."

"I hope you don't plan on running off on a sightseeing tour right away, Kathleen," Connor said. "The catalog is your first priority and can not be neglected."

Kathleen felt as she had many years ago, when a third-grade nun whacked her knuckles with a ruler for speaking out of turn. The sting was nothing compared to the embarrassment of being reprimanded by Connor. Her psyche had been extremely fragile as an eight-year-old, and she was surprised to find she was no less vulnerable right now.

"I never take responsibility lightly, Connor, but I assumed I would be allowed one day off before I leave this lovely land."

Connor's fork stopped in midair and clinked against his wine glass. Theresa's hand quickly masked her mouth, but her sparkling eyes revealed that she was tactfully concealing a smile.

"I didn't mean to sound censoring. I have a one-track mind right now, and it is totally focused on the new catalog. I'm sure that you will have time to visit your parents' hometown."

"After I have completed a rough draft of the catalog, you mean."

Connor nodded, and the threesome laughed.

"Perhaps I'll accompany you, Kathleen," Theresa said. "I'll be ready for a few days' relaxation by the end of the month."

"I'd like that."

After dessert, Connor asked if anyone would like an after-dinner drink. Before Kathleen could refuse, he took a crystal decanter from the sideboard.

Theresa spoke, her voice apologetic. "I hate to run off on your first night here, Kathleen, but I have a church meeting. Connor will see to it that you are entertained."

"I will be a most gracious host, rest assured, sister dear." Connor bowed his head. He would have tipped his hat if he had been wearing one, Kathleen thought, signaling the outer appearance of a courteous host. But no matter what he promised in the way of being gracious, she had her doubts.

"Shall we go inside for our drinks?"

Kathleen did not wish to spend another minute with Connor, especially alone, but to refuse would undoubtedly cause Theresa to skip her meeting. And perhaps she was being too sensitive. After all, he had tried to engage in friendly conversation. If only she felt more comfortable around him.

She followed him into the sitting room and sat on an upholstered chair beside the fireplace. The fire was blazing and painted the room with a warm golden glow.

Connor smiled; perhaps the role of host softened his attitude. Kathleen had an urge to reassure him of her ability to handle her job with Shea Crystal. She was willing to make concessions if it would ease the tension between them.

"Connor, I know how much it means to you for Shea Crystal to be successful in the American market. Capturing a sizable portion of the trade won't be easy since Waterford and a few French companies already have an edge. But with the proper approach, buyers should be able to recognize the quality and affordability of Shea glassware. I believe my background will help you reach that goal. It's an exciting prospect."

Connor studied Kathleen, considering her words. Soft honey hues flickered in his eyes, then disappeared, leaving dark agates in their place.

"It is a challenging project, Kathleen. One that must be attacked with all of our energies. I only hope you are prepared to dedicate every waking moment to Shea Crystal. Only then can we succeed."

Kathleen was stunned. His response had switched from a direct statement about the prospects for the American trade to an outright attack on her. She was not going to allow the remark to pass. She wouldn't let him think she was spineless.

"Why do you refuse to accept the fact that I may be right for this job?"

"Because I don't want an American meddling in our affairs, much less an American woman."

"That's absurd. And besides, Theresa is convinced that you need the input from an American."

"My sister has a peculiar way of rationalizing that what she wants is what Shea Crystal needs."

"Why didn't you refuse to go along with her if you feel so strongly about my being here? It would have saved us all a lot of grief."

"I don't know why. To placate her, perhaps. To end the arguments about who should fill the position. And now it appears I'm stuck with the decision."

"I can't accept that reason, Connor. You don't strike me as the type to be easily led about by someone else. You're angry because you didn't have input into the decision to hire me; your male ego has been bruised. If you were honest, you would admit that I'm qualified."

Connor turned away momentarily and Kathleen thought her words had hit the mark. Encouraged, she continued. "It was unfortunate that you missed the interview, but you have to realize that Theresa hired me because she was convinced that I could handle the job. And I can. Your sister didn't act on emotion; she's a shrewd businesswoman. And she wasn't trying to usurp your authority by acting on her own. She was confident that you would accept John Forbes' recommendation and my credentials."

"Perhaps."

"No two ways about it. Choosing an American to create the advertising strategy that will herald your crystal's introduction to the States makes sense. Why can't you acknowledge that instead of being so stubborn?"

"Perhaps I can't discard the belief that pretty young ladies should attend to ladies' work."

"You don't mean that! That line went out with wringer washing machines. You spent enough time in my country to realize that the barriers have been dropped. People should be judged on ability, not hindered by gender. And by the looks of your own sister's position at Shea Crystal, it's obvious that you are merely giving lip service to old prejudices.

"We seem to have a real personality conflict here, and I don't know what caused it. If we're going to work together, we have to come to a truce. Otherwise my effectiveness is going to be hampered. If that happens, Shea Crystal will be the loser."

Connor stepped closer to the fire, and bent to warm his hands in front of the hearth. Kathleen presumed it was a delaying tactic while he considered how to answer her. He jammed his hands into his pants pockets and took a casual stance.

"You're probably right; I am being rigid. I'm having a hard time accepting the idea of hiring an outsider, and then to be edged out of the final decision, really irked me. However, I was blaming you for a situation not of your making. You want to be judged by your ability, and that's only right. So, Kathleen, prove yourself with the preliminary work on the catalog, and I won't give you any more trouble."

"Fair enough, Connor, fair enough. Now, if you'll excuse me, I'm going upstairs to bed. I'm still jet-lagged, and I want to get an early start in the morning."

"Good night, Kathleen."

Kathleen walked up to her room, her thoughts running at a marathon pace. She vowed to produce copy and layouts superior to anything Connor had ever seen. She would prove herself, all right. He would regret ever doubting her. He would beg her forgiveness! Beg? Connor O'Shea? Not on her life. Cold doubt began to slither into place, edging out her confidence. She considered herself a first-rate advertising person, not a genius. Her creativity had limits. Faced with the perfectionist expectations of Connor O'Shea, she had to admit that being darned good might not be good enough.

Chapter Four

Kathleen woke to a mist-shrouded morning that diffused the sunlight outside her window. Memories of her first day in Ireland were a kaleidoscope—color and form whirling into jagged shapes, then exploding into fragments. Some of the pieces evoked pastel memories of the countryside, while vivid red and purple painted harsh sketches of her conflict with Connor.

She threw off the comforter and swung her legs over the side of the bed. Pushing aside a stray lock of hair that fluttered across her forehead, Kathleen fought the butterfly swarm that gathered in her stomach. She had to face Connor O'Shea this morning, at the breakfast table or the glassworks. He was on home turf; she was a stranger intruding on his territory. He had made that clear.

After showering, she put on a tweed pants outfit. She hoped to present a professional appearance at the glassworks without sacrificing femininity.

She stood in front of the mirror and critically assessed her appearance. The mottled gray pants were stovepipe slim; the short jacket and silk blouse complimented the tailored look. Misty green eyes were framed by thick lashes and her softly curled copper hair grazed her shoulders.

When she was a child, Kathleen had detested her hair. She constantly had to parry nicknames—Red or Scarlet—that the other kids unmercifully tagged her with. Her hair was an asset now. Glowing with silken luster, it gave brilliance to her milky complexion.

"You look self-possessed and successful," she informed the mirrored reflection. "Just act that way and everyone will believe it, too."

The pep talk did not do much to bolster her confidence. She put her hands over her face as a wave of anxiety washed over her. This was silly. She was a professional. She could stand up for herself; she would survive.

She could no longer put off going downstairs. Whether or not it had been a good choice to accept the job here, she was stuck with it. On the practical side, odds were that she would have had to endure an unpleasant, bullying employer at some time during her career. She had been lucky in the past but now the odds had caught up with her. She would do her best and try to consider it a challenge.

A challenge? She smiled to herself as she walked into the breakfast alcove. That was a new spin.

Jennie bustled into the room bearing a teapot and a plate of warm soda bread. It was obvious from her quick appearance that she had been listening for sounds of Kathleen's approach.

"Did Theresa have breakfast yet?" Kathleen asked.

"Oh, yes, Miss. She's at the glassworks. As is Himself."

"Himself?"

"Mr. Connor."

Kathleen allowed herself the luxury of a smile. Himself: it was a good description of the lord of the manor.

"I'll have your plate in a moment," Jennie said. "Would you like a bowl of flakes?"

Corn flakes, Kathleen reasoned, declining.

The tea was strong. She removed the lid from the pot and was horrified to see half a dozen tea bags darkening the brew. No wonder they had to water the beverage down with milk. Right now it was strong enough to cure hoof and mouth disease. She would have to remember to tell Jennie she preferred weak tea.

Immediately after breakfast Kathleen left for the factory. It seemed early but the absence of Connor and Theresa made her wonder if she were late. She chided herself for forgetting to adjust her watch to the time change. Couldn't she do anything right?

Gunmetal gray clouds dulled the sky and the air was chill. Kathleen gripped the lapels of her blazer and pulled them together in an effort to seal out the cold. California's temperate climate had not prepared her for this. Even San Francisco's morning fog was more welcome than the frosty tendrils that plucked at her body, robbing it of heat.

It couldn't be any colder than the reception that awaited her at Shea Crystal, she mused. *Try to think of the bright side,* Kathleen told herself. Connor might be too busy to notice her.

She walked through the parking lot and was dismayed to see that there were about as many cars and bicycles as the previous day. There was no denying that she was late. She hurried, yanked open the lobby door and rushed inside.

"Good morning, Kathleen," Clare Kelly called out.

"Hello, Clare. Am I late?"

"We start at half past eight."

It was said without hint of censure, but the clock above the receptionist's desk indicated it was nearly nine o'clock. She gave Clare a weak smile and quickly walked to Theresa's office.

Theresa looked up from her typing when Kathleen entered the room.

"My first full day on the job and I'm not on time. I'm so embarrassed. I didn't think to change my watch."

"Don't be concerned, everyone experiences jet-lag after a transatlantic flight. No one will fault you for being a few minutes late.

"We've arranged an office for you. It isn't much, but I thought it would be preferable to sharing space with one of us."

Especially if that "one" was Connor, Kathleen thought.

They walked down the hall and Theresa led Kathleen into a small but well-lighted room. A worn desk, chair and drawing board were the only furnishings.

"Sean is scavenging around for a typewriter. Let me know if there is anything else you need and we can have it for you in a matter of days."

Kathleen hadn't used a typewriter in years. Harris and Forbes had computer work stations at every desk. She was thankful that she'd had the foresight to bring her laptop with her.

"I won't need a typewriter, Theresa. I brought my computer."

"A computer . . . ?" Theresa shook her head, as though the word conjured a foreign image.

"I will need a printer and a scanner, however. If

that's a problem, I can see about having mine shipped out."

"Give Sean the specifications and he can call one of the Galway computer stores. I thought you might like to go through some recent catalogs and see what we've been doing. Not that I want you to be influenced by someone else's work, but it will acquaint you with our crystal."

"Who is in charge of your domestic catalog?"

"A firm in Galway. We've never had reason to have our own advertising staff. While you work on the American catalog, the Galway firm will continue to handle our other needs. If we are successful with the American trade and, perhaps, acquire a line of china, it will be necessary to increase advertising. Then we may consider developing an in-house advertising staff.

"Your catalog will be a forerunner, the first produced within our walls. After the project is completed, I hope you'll think about remaining in Ireland to take charge."

"You certainly trust blind faith, Theresa. Although I don't doubt my ability to create a quality catalog, it's obvious that I'm going to run into opposition from your brother. He may be dissatisfied with every piece of copy and layout I turn in."

"My brother comes on strong at times, and he is less than tactful about his displeasure with my decision to hire an American. Connor's obstinate, I'll grant you, but don't let that discourage you. Once he sees the results of a fresh approach to this advertising scheme, he'll come around. Connor is a good man, and he's fair, even though he is not showing his finest side right now."

Theresa fumbled with the tray of pencils on the desk, obviously uncomfortable discussing her brother on a personal level. Kathleen sensed that she was not one to be cut into separate parts. Just as one of Connor's strongest traits was a fierce allegiance to his countrymen, Theresa's might well be her loyalty to her brother.

After Theresa left, the tiny office became too quiet, ominously devoid of sound. Kathleen browsed through the desk that would be hers during her stay at Shea Crystal. It contained the usual semblance of tools that a copywriter and graphic artist might need. It was not an up-to-date arrangement; Kathleen was accustomed to sitting at a computer terminal to compose copy and calling upon state-of-the-art software for layouts. If she stayed on, she would have to discuss upgrading facilities. Stayed on? She'd be lucky to last the day.

The rest of the morning was spent poring over the catalogs Theresa had provided. The copy was sterile and unimaginative, but the layouts were professional. The crystal was exquisite, and the right advertising campaign could place it in front of hundreds of thousands of new consumers. But the trick was to win over department-store buyers. If they didn't send in orders, the American public would remain ignorant of the splendid Irish crystal.

A few minutes before noon, Kathleen went to the display room. She wanted to touch the glass, feel the symmetry, press her fingertips into the deep grooves. She had to get to know each pattern intimately before she could persuade others to hold it in their hands.

In her second look at the cascades of shimmering crystal she was as entranced with the sight as she had been the day before. The O'Sheas had a right to be proud of the goblets, vases and decanters wrought from fire and earth.

The door swung open and Theresa marched in, followed by a dozen or so people. She sidled up to Kathleen and whispered, "Slip out before you get caught in this boring tour. Connor is firing glass, I think you will find it interesting."

Kathleen nodded. Although she knew the tour would not be boring, she did not contradict Theresa.

Reaching the entrance to the heart of the glassworks, she hesitated. Should she observe Connor at work, as his sister had directed? She did not wish to have another confrontation with him, but on the other hand, how would she explain to Theresa that she had ignored her suggestion?

She pulled open the door and was stunned by the blast of sight and sound. The room was a melange of motion and color. Activity centered around black furnaces with golden souls. Kathleen scanned the glassblowers and their apprentices until her gaze found Connor. Chest bare, his discarded shirt trailed from the waistband of his pants. He worked beside a blazing furnace and silver beads of perspiration glistened across his skin.

When she approached his work area, he seemed to sense her presence and he looked up. Their eyes met and an electric sensation brushed her skin.

He held a long steel rod with molten glass bulging at the tip. His hands embraced the tube, his slender fingers arching as he slowly turned it. She followed the movement, watching the sinews ripple along his biceps, the muscles expand and contract across his sweat-drenched chest. There was primitive power in his stance.

The glass took on a golden hue, urged into shape by the heat infused by man and fire. A beautiful crystal decanter was being born from Connor's hands and breath.

Connor's eyes were as hot as the flames that danced in the furnace. His gaze never left her face, but she was unable to read his expression.

Connor rested the decanter on a pad and turned it, shaping the slender neck, then with an unexpected move, he plunged the glass into a bucket of cold water. Steam hissed and swirled as the glass cooled into hardness.

Connor handed the rod with the decanter to an apprentice, who broke the neck free of the tube. He stepped down from the platform and struggled into his shirt, his arm sweeping against Kathleen's shoulder. She felt the warmth he had absorbed from the fire and unsuccessfully fought to repress the tension that plucked at her nerve endings. She could think of nothing clever to say to cover her unsettled emotions, so she clamped her teeth tightly to prevent an inane remark from escaping.

"I'm surprised to see you here." His fingers closed around her arm as he led her away from the platform.

"Theresa suggested I watch you work; I couldn't very well refuse." She knew she sounded remote, but it was safer than allowing the conversation to become personal.

"Were you impressed?" Connor's mouth curved into a taunting smile.

"Yes. I've never been inside a glassworks before. The way you manipulated that glass was amazing."

"Come, I'll show you how the crystal is cut."

He did not relinquish his grip on her arm and the heady effect his closeness produced nearly made her stumble. To pull away would be childish, but somehow he seemed more of an adversary when he was friendly than when he was angry. She could fight anger with harsh words, but this unexpected emotion was something she was unprepared for.

The hum of power tools filled the cutting room. They walked to a cubicle where a cutter was working on champagne flutes. He checked the pencil marks outlining the design before pressing the glass to a powersaw with a tiny copper blade. With deft movements he turned the glass until each facet was cut.

"Our workers are paid by the piece, but quality is never compromised for quantity. We don't sell seconds; imperfect glass is destroyed." Pride sounded in Connor's voice.

It was obvious that Shea Crystal was integral to his life. Kathleen sensed that the goals he set for himself were even more demanding than those he pressed on others.

"He's working on one of our most popular patterns, 'Thistledown.' " Connor nodded toward the cutter. "It looks a bit dirty in this stage; it still has to be polished with pumice to remove the grit."

"It's exquisite, Connor. I'm sure it will be popular in the States."

Connor released his grip on Kathleen's arm. His eyes became clouded.

"I have work to do. Can you find your way back?"

She was stunned by the sudden change. Was it her reference to America that wrenched him away from being a hospitable tour guide? Was the reminder that she would be working for him so devastating?

"I can find my way back, Connor. Although, I would have thought, as head of a company as prestigious as Shea Crystal, you might have accumulated a set of manners somewhere along the way."

She felt a pang of satisfaction at the surprise that registered on his face. Connor O'Shea had better beware if he planned to treat her with a constant lack of regard.

But he chose not to answer. A scowl crossed his face, his eyes darkened and he whirled, quickly putting distance between them.

"You're rude," she called after him, knowing that the buzz of power tools muted her words so that only she heard them. It didn't matter. She knew her reproach would have had no impact on Connor, anyway.

Chapter Five

Kathleen returned to her office. The lack of space was suddenly oppressive, but she knew that the thoughts about Connor that crowded her mind were responsible for the suffocating feeling.

His abrupt mood change was disturbing. While they were on neutral ground in their appreciation of fine crystal, Connor had appeared eager to give her the grand tour. What had caused him to switch from amiable host to hostile stranger? Kathleen couldn't tolerate being spoken to politely one minute and raged at the next.

She had to rid herself of this growing agitation. If she couldn't remedy the discord between Connor and herself, at least she could ease the tight band around her head that threatened to burst into a vicious headache. She needed a walk, some tension-breaking exercise, but did not feel comfortable leaving her desk since she was new to the job.

There was no running away from her position at Shea Crystal. Even if she and Connor constantly batted heads, she was locked into the job for at least six weeks. Two strong motives tied her to this foreign land: a moral commitment to keep her word and the necessity to repair her financial predicament.

John Forbes had not been the only one to invest in Brian's dreams—or schemes. She had loaned him five thousand dollars, her entire savings, to help get his idea off the ground. He had promised repayment with interest, but she realized now that there was slim chance of ever seeing the money or Brian again. She had been had, and it rankled.

She hoped that putting distance between herself and all that had disrupted her life might smooth the edges of her disappointments. At least here, she didn't have to field questions about Brian. And maybe eventually she would stop questioning herself.

Brian. What a paradox. His sales record at Harris and Forbes had surpassed all the other reps. John Forbes had confided that he was considering a partnership for Brian when the tableware contract was signed. Kathleen had been proud of Brian. Their friendship had grown and she had nearly given him her heart. They had been very close and Brian sometimes spoke of his aspirations.

They were somewhat lofty, yet not unusual for an ambitious person. They discussed her career options and goals, but she had been hesitant to say much about what she expected beyond that. She wanted marriage and children, but she could not imagine herself as Mrs. Brian Thomas, despite the attraction between them. Although they were considered a couple, neither had spoken words of love. She was thankful for that.

But that was in the past; she must now focus her time and energy on Shea Crystal. A new start, a clean slate was offered here and no matter what irritations accompanied that, it was her best hope.

Things had moved so quickly, there was an unreal quality to being in Ireland. One day she was sipping a latté and rushing to catch a cable car, the next she was thousands of miles away, with an ocean separating her old life from her new.

It seemed strange not to have a friend nearby, someone to share her doubts and perhaps offer encouragement in return. The time difference was huge enough to prevent picking up the phone and dialing San Francisco. She was isolated, not just by the geography of Achill Island.

While her inner strengths had always been enough, she wondered if they would see her through now. She wondered, too, if she could prevail against a man who was prejudiced against her. Her ability in advertising was not the issue; he simply did not want her in the job.

Connor was locked into an inflexible preconception and she doubted that he would admit that he had been rash in his appraisal. He wanted to be right.

It was important to convince him that she was not a threat to the status quo at Land's End or Shea Crystal. Her intrusion did not herald a sorority. She smiled at the analogy. She could visualize Connor surrounded by a female sales force, female glass blowers and cutters. He would make up for his lack of affirmative action in one swoop.

Enough silliness, she thought, forcing her attention back to work, writing rough copy and outlining tentative layouts for one of the patterns. But concentration was fragmentary. Her thoughts continued to drift back to Connor.

At quitting time, she was still bristling with nervous energy. Unless she found an activity to consume her restlessness, she would be a wreck by dinnertime. A horseback ride might be just the thing.

Theresa was more than happy to show her the Connemaras. She was hesitant about Kathleen riding alone but Kathleen pointed out that it would be nearly impossible to get lost if she rode along the beach.

They picked up the tack from a lean-to and walked to the pasture together. Theresa seemed caught in a sentimental mood as she spoke of the horses.

"When Father was alive, we exhibited at the Connemara Fair and the Dublin Horse Show. Connor and I rode in dressage classes and we took home our share of ribbons. Now, I hardly have time to exercise my mare enough to keep her from going to fat."

There was a wistful quality in Theresa's voice and Kathleen sensed that she missed life as it was before her parents' deaths. Perhaps she would not have taken an active role in Shea Crystal if fate had not changed the path of her life. Ironic, that the responsibility Theresa considered too weighty, was the goal Kathleen was working toward.

"I wish I had Connor's energy, but I don't."

The mention of Connor's name renewed Kathleen's uneasiness. It was because of him that she needed to ride, to wear off tension.

A pair of horses grazed close together, oblivious to the women. On the other side of the fence, in a separate pasture, a powerfully built gray watched attentively. He threw his head impatiently and whinnied, then trotted across the field, muscles rippling beneath a mottled silver coat.

"That's Baron, Connor's horse."

It was a magnificent steed, about sixteen hands,

with excellent conformation. As a chestnut mare ambled toward the women, the gray whinnied possessively, seemingly entreating the other horse to turn away from the humans. Domineering as the master, Kathleen mused. What a wonderful ride he would provide!

Kathleen had been riding since she was twelve, advancing from beginning equitation to hunter classes. Although she could not boast a wall full of ribbons, she had won a cup for jumping when she was in high school. Her parents had been so proud, they leased a horse for the entire summer and she had spent every waking moment at the stables. It was the next best thing to owning her own horse and she had reveled in the joy of it.

After graduation, college and a part-time job consumed all of her attention. Kathleen made up for lost time after she became established with Harris and Forbes. She went horseback riding through Golden Gate Park every weekend, and in the Sierras on summer vacations.

"I must get back to the house, Sean is coming by . . . business, of course." Theresa's face colored. "You're welcome to ride my mare. She has a sweet disposition and smooth gait. I'll see you at dinner."

Kathleen watched Connor's sister as she walked across the field toward the house. Her shoulders crowded forward and her pace was slow and heavy. She worked too hard, undoubtedly forced into overachieving by Connor's pace. It wasn't fair that his own drive for success should be imposed on his sister. Theresa should have the gumption to stand up to her brother. But then, there was more to it than assertiveness. Connor's sister probably was tied to a social code that was difficult to break.

Kathleen heaved the saddle and blanket onto the rock wall. Theresa's mare had returned to grazing. The chestnut's belly was a bit too rounded. As Theresa had indicated, the horse wasn't getting enough exercise. But the gray was not suffering from lack of a rider; that was evident in its sleek lines. It would be thrilling to ride the animal.

Would it be all right to take Connor's horse? Theresa hadn't said Baron was off limits.

Scrambling over the fence, she yanked a tuft of grass from the ground and extended it to the horse, crooning softly as she inched closer.

The gray snorted and reared, its hooves flailing the air. Kathleen stepped back, momentarily frightened, but her decision to ride the animal did not waver. The gray quieted, muscles quivering beneath a silken coat. The horse's nostrils flared, its pose attentive as it observed Kathleen's approach. She could not contain her excitement.

She slipped the bridle over the horse's head and pressed the bit into its mouth. It did not resist, but the bright eyes and rippling muscles spoke of only temporary restraint.

After saddling up, she slipped her foot into the stirrup and mounted. The horse communicated impatience by chewing at the bit and prancing. Although Baron matched her own mood, Kathleen intended to keep the horse in check. Just as a swimmer would not dive into a strange pond before testing the water, neither would she be fool enough to give an unfamiliar horse its head.

She opened the pasture gate and kicked it shut after the horse went through. The mare whinnied after them, sounding forlorn at being left behind. Or relieved? Kathleen smiled.

The beach stretched unspoiled, free of bodies or litter found at so many California bathing areas. Kathleen pressed her heels against the horse's sides and the gray responded, breaking into a trot, then lengthening the stride into a smooth canter.

Kathleen and Baron were in perfect harmony, attuned to one another's signals. All the anxieties that had plagued her fell away in response to the freedom of riding Connor's horse.

She took in her surroundings, like a tourist. The late afternoon sun's rays spread wings of silver across the emerald water. The waves appeared to be edged with ecru lace as they crested and broke against a golden ribbon of sand that curved gracefully into infinity.

Lavender heather and buttercup yellow Scotch broom cascaded over stone walls enclosing the meadows. Farther along, sheep grazed peacefully, seemingly unaware of anything but the need to feed.

Kathleen come upon a tumble-down stone shack, pieces of its thatched roof a nesting place for birds. She slowed the horse and studied the abandoned cottage. The center of the roof and the two side walls had crumbled, providing a dollhouse-view of the interior. A wide chimney clung to one wall. Its hearth, now filled with rubble, had once been the hub of the spartan home.

Throwing his head back and forth, nearly yanking the reins from Kathleen's grip, Baron communicated impatience. She loosened her hold on the reins, yielding to the animal's desire to run. Leaning forward, she gave the horse its head. The pace increased until the horse was running flat out and sand exploded from beneath its hooves. Kathleen caught her fingers through the mane, her face so close to Baron's neck, the rough hair was like sandpaper against her cheeks.

The salt air slapped her face and brought stinging tears to her eyes. She wiped the dampness with the back of her hand and brushed a stray fall of hair from her forehead. Perspiration mixed with seawater dampened the horse's flesh and formed tiny beads that flew against Kathleen's cheeks.

Suddenly the sound of another horse intruded. Thudding hooves signalled that another rider was breaching the distance. Kathleen was no longer alone.

She twisted in the saddle to see who was pursuing her, but her vision was blurred by tears pressed upon her by the wind. Her heartbeat quickened. Had she been foolhardy to ride alone? Was there as much danger lurking on this solitary island as there was in the heart of a big city? Her heels dug into Baron's side, urging the horse to lengthen its stride. The horse snorted, throwing its head and fighting to get the bit between its teeth.

Two fears battled for priority: Kathleen was frightened of the stranger pursuing her and fearful that she might lose control of her mount. The hoof-beats that followed were coming closer. No matter how much Baron's speed increased, the other horse continued to challenge.

Suddenly, the reins were torn from her grip and Baron crowhopped in rebellion, nearly throwing her. She screamed. Her heartbeat hammered at her breast, causing her breath to knot painfully in her throat.

A strong arm flashed around her waist and yanked her off the horse. Her legs beat the air and defensively, she fought to gain purchase on the other horse, fearful she would fall to the ground and be trampled. Clinging to the assailant's shoulder, her vision blurred by windwhipped tears, she threw a leg over the other horse's rump.

She fell forward, her face pressed against the muscled back of her captor. Instinctively, she flung her arms around him to keep from falling.

Panic subsided; she recognized the fabric of her captor's shirt, the musky scent of his aftershave.

It was Connor!

"Put me down, darn you!"

Connor reined the horse in and as the animal slowed to a trot, Kathleen felt a surge of courage. Her hands became tight little fists and she pounded Connor's back, her internal fury transformed into physical force.

"Put me down, Connor!"

Connor swung a leg over the pommel and slid to the ground. He stood for a moment, his legs apart in an arrogant posture, his eyes dark. Then he reached for Kathleen and before she could protest that she didn't need help, pulled her from the horse.

She felt the coarseness of his shirt, his muscled chest as he drew her to the ground. Her legs were unsteady and she fought a dizzy sensation.

"Are you all right?"

The question was ludicrous. "What do you mean, 'all right?' After you wrenched me from the horse? Almost caused me to be trampled underfoot?" Her face was flushed; she could feel the heat of anger and frustration.

"You had no business riding Baron; he's too

much horse. He was out of control. I had to stop him."

"You were the only one out of control, Connor. For whatever twisted reason, you decided to humiliate me."

"Baron's a stallion, Kathleen. If you'd come upon a mare in season, Baron would have gone crazy—you could have been hurt."

"You weren't worried about me, Connor," she lashed out. "You were just playing macho-man. Next time, pick on someone your own size."

Connor grabbed the gray's reins—*his* horse—and swung into the saddle. He pierced Kathleen with a dark look, and slapped the reins against the stallion's side. The horse reared, its forelegs beating the air, then it leaped forward and broke into a canter, its hooves spraying sand at Kathleen.

"Go on, take your darned horse, take your anger, but don't ever try to bully me again!"

Venting her frustration at Connor's retreating back brought little satisfaction. Kathleen knew that the words did not ring true, not to Connor, if he could hear them, or to herself.

Chapter Six

Kathleen swung into the saddle. The leather was still warm.

When she reached the pasture, she dismounted and brought the horse through the gate. Connor's stallion was grazing on the other side of the fence, as though it had never left the meadow. It was difficult to believe such a volatile scene had taken place because she had chosen to ride the animal.

She removed the horse's tack and picked up a currycomb from the lean-to. The horse's coat was crusted with sweat and she vigorously worked at brushing it, her anger flowing into the movements.

Finished, Kathleen smacked the horse's rump to signal it to return to grazing. The animal responded by kicking its heels and whinnying to the others, but they did not even raise their heads. *Horses are as oblique as their owner*, Kathleen mused.

She returned to the house and found Theresa pacing the living room. She appeared distressed.

"I'm glad you're back."

"What's the matter, Theresa?"

"I have an appointment with Sean, but it conflicts with a business dinner I'm scheduled to attend with Connor. I don't know how I could have forgotten . . ." Her hands carved a mindless arc in the air. "I wouldn't ask . . . but Sean will be furious if I cancel another engagement with him."

"Slow down, Theresa. I don't know what you're trying to tell me."

"Will you take my place and go with Connor?" Theresa's brows knitted together in a pleading gesture.

"Me? Oh, I don't think so. Connor and I don't get along, you know that."

"We're obligated to have two people from Shea Crystal attend. Please, Kathleen."

"I . . ." She dreaded the thought of leaving herself open to another stormy scene, even for Theresa's sake.

"I wouldn't ask if it didn't mean a great deal to me. Sean and I have been seeing one another and it's been a strain trying to balance my personal life with the business. I can't seem to make anyone happy, and I don't want to be forced into making a choice. I'm not ready. Not yet."

"All right, Theresa. But your brother is not going to appreciate the change in plans. We had a disturbing encounter while I was out riding that may make it difficult for us to be civil dinner partners."

"I see." Theresa cast her eyes downward and clasped her hands together. Her shoulders sagged and she shook her head slowly. "Then I can't impose upon you."

"No, no. You go ahead with your plans. If Connor says anything disagreeable I'll grit my teeth. I won't give him an opportunity to take offense at anything I say. And maybe you're right—it might turn out to be an enjoyable evening." Kathleen smiled. She knew her words sounded sincere, even though she didn't believe them.

"Thank you, Kathleen. I'll make it up to you."

"That isn't necessary, Theresa."

"I'm glad you came to Ireland . . . so very glad," Theresa said softly, before she turned and walked away.

Kathleen valued the friendship that was developing with Theresa and was glad she could help her out of a tight spot. But it placed her in a precarious position. There was slim chance that the evening would run smoothly, but it was too late to allow her anxieties to change the course of events. She had given her word and was committed to seeing it through.

Kathleen went upstairs to clean up. In the shower, she turned on the knobs and was exasperated with the lazy flow of water. It was more like a garden sprinkling can than a shower. Afterward, she toweled herself briskly and put on a simple ivory-colored dress that flattered her slender figure and was appropriate for any occasion.

Theresa had neglected to tell Kathleen what time her brother expected her to be ready, but since Connor wasn't pounding on the bedroom door, she doubted that he was being kept waiting.

Determined not to antagonize him tonight, even if it meant swallowing her pride, peace at any cost was her goal. Connor would look petty if he maintained anger while she was pleasant.

She tucked a stray hair into place and felt her hand tremble against her scalp.

As she walked downstairs and into the sitting room, Kathleen attempted to compose herself. The fire was burning gently, a soft reminder of the certainty of a chill evening. The flames swayed together like lovers locked in an embrace, then split apart only to twist together again.

She turned away. Why did an innocuous hearth fire make her think of romance? And why had a lightning-quick image of Connor flashed through her mind?

"I'm surprised you would agree to go out with me tonight."

Kathleen whirled. It was as though her thoughts had conjured him.

"You look lovely. That dress is very flattering."

"Thank you."

The compliment caught her off guard. The planes of Connor's face softened and Kathleen was relieved that the storm clouds had cleared, at least for the moment.

They left the house and climbed into the Volvo. A short distance down the road they were slowed to a halt by a herd of cows. A farmer prodded the last animal with a gnarled stick but it seemed as though his action was prompted by habit rather than a need to hurry the herd.

"I don't believe it!" Kathleen exclaimed. "Surely there are laws against blocking the road like this."

"Don't be so impatient, lass. They have the right of way. They'll move out of our path in their own good time, not one minute sooner."

Kathleen envisioned a cable car hurtling along O'Farrell Street and being halted by half a dozen indolent cows on their way to market. The conductor's arm would ache from yanking the bell cord but the cows would ignore the clanging and would "move in their own good time, not one minute sooner!"

"What's so funny?" Connor asked.

"I was thinking how differently San Franciscans would view a delay in their commute."

Connor made up for lost time by driving fifty miles an hour along the narrow, curving roadway. Kathleen clutched the armrest on the door. It was unsettling enough to drive on the wrong side of the road at breakneck speed, but this ribbon of roadway couldn't possibly accommodate two cars at the same time. She feared what would happen if a vehicle came from the other direction.

"Aren't we going too fast?" Her knuckles were pale from the pressure of her grip on the armrest.

"Relax, Kathleen, I know these roads."

His confidence did not calm her nerves. The Volvo's speed should be reserved for a freeway, not a country throroughfare shared with bovines. She had to admit that one thing was on their side—the absence of other motorists.

They crossed the bridge that separated Achill Island from the mainland and the road became busier. Cars hurtled along at a crazy pace. For a moment, Kathleen closed her eyes, leaned back and took a deep breath. Would she ever cease feeling queasy about seeing a car race toward them on what she perceived to be their side of the road?

She forced her concentration on the pastoral scenery. The rolling farmland, interrupted by an occasional brick or cinderblock house, was a patchwork of grassy fields fringed with buttercup-colored thickets.

"There's Croagh Patrick," Connor pointed to a cone-like mountain. "The very spot where St. Patrick drove the snakes from Ireland and brought the people the gift of faith."

"Croagh Patrick! My mother told me she made a yearly trek up the mountain with her convent school."

"With or without shoes?" Conner asked.

"Mother was too sensible to go barefoot. She told me that on her last pilgrimage, the sight of an old man with bleeding feet made her turn back."

"Sometimes hardship strengthens a person. It's one of the secrets of why the Irish endure. We're a stubborn lot; nothing undermines our determination."

Kathleen searched for a veiled allusion to their situation but Connor's expression was open.

They approached a serpentine waterway. Waves gently lapped at the sandy edges of meadowland. A scattering of houses were built along a rise. It was unlike California, where urban sprawl would have gobbled up every fifty-foot lot bordering bay and hillside; sun-worshippers in quest of waterfront or view property.

"That's Clew Bay, a favorite spot for salmon fishing. We're in Westport," Connor said. "Westport is a popular vacation resort."

Westport! Kathleen's mother's family had summered here, riding the train to the seaside village. Theresa had been right, everything was close. It would be easy for Kathleen to trace her family's history while staying at Land's End.

The pungent aroma of cows, corn and alfalfa was more enticing than any perfume bottled by Halston or Chanel. The sights and scents gave new dimension to her mother's stories.

Connor turned the car onto a private road and up a steep hill to a two-story house that faced the bay. A discreet sign read "Ardmore House."

"Here we are." He turned and smiled, the only indication of friendship he had offered since he was told Kathleen would be working for him.

Inside the restaurant, the hostess greeted Connor with respectful recognition; he was not a newcomer to the small family dinner house. She led them to a secluded window alcove with a view of Clew Bay and took their orders for curried chicken before disappearing.

"Are we early?" Kathleen asked.

"I forgot to tell you of the change in plans." He leaned across the table and gazed at her, his eyes molten gold. "You looked so lovely, I couldn't bear to tell you that the meeting was postponed."

"Why didn't you say something sooner?"

"I was afraid you would turn down a personal

invitation, and I wouldn't have blamed you. I wanted a chance to apologize for this afternoon."

She had tried to push aside the traumatic termination of her afternoon ride, urge it into a dark recess of her memory until it was forgotten like the cobwebs that cluttered the corners of an unused room. But that wouldn't solve anything.

"Your actions this afternoon were terrible. I'm an employee and a guest in your home, yet you treated me badly. I want your respect; and I want to respect you, otherwise we will continue to be at odds with one another. And that's not good for productivity."

Connor was poised to reply, but Kathleen raised her hand, palm out, to signal her desire to continue to have the stage. He leaned back in his chair and did not interrupt.

"You've been hitting me on two levels, personal and professional. If you continue to jab at my ability as an advertising person, you're going to slow me down, but I'll still accomplish what I set out to. It will simply take longer. If you decimate my confidence in myself, that's another matter."

"You're right, of course. Try to believe me when I say that I was concerned with your safety this afternoon. When I realized you were riding Baron, all sorts of horrid scenes raced through my mind. I imagined you lying in a bog or worse. I had no idea that you were an accomplished rider. I'm sorry I was rough in my 'rescue'."

"I accept your apology. Now what about about my work?"

"I looked at your portfolio before I left the factory today. The copy is crisp and original. I think you're going to be okay, Kathleen Flaherty. More than okay. Now, let's enjoy the fine food and view," he said as the waitress placed their plates in front of them.

Kathleen was relieved at the truce. Her stomach no longer churned in response to the tensions that had erupted sporadically since she arrived in Ireland. She felt calm now; she had aired her complaints, and Connor had allayed her anxieties. Perhaps they could work together in harmony.

She tasted her food and was pleased with the light curry flavor. They ate in semi-silence, each caught up in separate thoughts. When they finished their meal, coffee was served with a plate of cookies. Kathleen sipped the dark brew and stared out the window. Clew Bay was postcard lovely as the last lingering rays of sunlight pressed golden spears across the quivering water.

"What are you thinking about?" Connor asked.

"I was remembering a snapshot of my mother taken in Westport. She was at the beach in a bloomered swimsuit, struggling with an oversized wicker picnic hamper. Grandmother carried an umbrella to ward off sunburn. Grandfather was in the picture, too, toting his fishing gear. Mother said he prided himself on catching enough salmon to share with the neighbors."

"We have something in common. My father spent many hours fly-casting along the loch. But he didn't often provide a fresh fish dinner, unless it was straight from the butcher."

Kathleen smiled. At the moment, she was completely relaxed in Connor's company. Perhaps he wasn't quite the ogre she had thought. Not that she was naive enough to believe there would be no more confrontations or flaring tempers. In a high-stress job, there were bound to be setbacks. She pushed those thoughts aside. She wanted to enjoy the tranquil mood that now prevailed, but wondered how long it would last.

She would try to remain optimistic about her future with Shea Crystal. After all, Connor had conceded her competence as a copywriter. That was a start in the right direction.

Chapter Seven

From Kathleen's bedroom window the next morning, the sky appeared tinged with an emerald hue, a reflection, perhaps of her own green eyes.

She saw things differently today. Connor's acceptance of her last night, his words of encouragement about the copy she'd written, changed her view of everything—work, this foreign land, and the man himself. Trepidation about the decision to be on Shea Crystal's staff was lessened. For the first time since accepting the job, she felt buoyant, excited about the opportunity to see Ireland, grateful for being on Shea Crystal's payroll.

Like a cat, she arched her back and stretched, long and lean, before getting out of bed. She whirled around the room like a ballerina; a weight had been lifted from her shoulders. Finally, Connor judged her by performance, not stereotype. Even though she sensed their truce was conditional, it was a start. She would settle for that.

She bristled with energy and could hardly wait to get to her desk and compose the kind of copy that had gained her a reputation at Harris and Forbes. Gone were the demons that had chased her.

There was one snag. A complication she had not anticipated: a strong attraction to Connor. How had it happened? Wasn't he the antithesis of what she wanted in a man: bullying, obstinate, tactless? But last night another side had emerged, sensitive and open. She respected his determination—she had a fair share of that herself—and his loyalty. Treasuring the significance of family roots her parents had instilled in her, she appreciated his committment to carry on family traditions.

Yes, she mused, Connor's positive attributes outnumbered the negative qualities. But, to be honest with herself, it wasn't character that intrigued her, it was something more—a strong physical pull.

With a little encouragement, he probably would have kissed her last night. It had been tempting. She wondered what it would have been like to find herself in his embrace, his lips pressed against hers. A bit of regret nagged at her.

But he was her boss. Until she'd met Brian, she had stuck to the tried-and-true code of not dating anyone she worked with. Brian's charm had dazzled her and she had tossed the rules out the window. A fast learner, she did not intend to repeat the mistake. Imagine how much more tangled things would be if she got involved with the boss and the relationship bombed?

But how long could she postpone the inevitable? If they worked side by side at Shea Crystal, the magnetism would grow stronger.

Worry about that when you get to it, she told herself.

In the meantime, she had goals to set and a completion date that was frightening. There was no room for mistakes or setbacks, no emergency escape clause. She was facing Challenge with a capital C.

Fifteen minutes later, Kathleen went down for breakfast and discovered that Connor and Theresa had beat her to work again. She poured a cup of coffee, gulped it and then hurried from the house. She practically sprinted to the glassworks.

Outside Connor's office she became apprehensive. She fiddled with her blouse, running her fingers along the placket, fastening the top button, then tucking the tails into her slacks rather than wearing it loosely fitted. Delaying tactics.

Would Connor see right through her business-like facade and know that she was smitten? But she had kept a proper distance last night, she reminded herself. Nothing in her demeanor had suggested compromising her position with the boss. Reassured, she pushed the door open and walked inside.

Connor was talking to someone and he turned in surprise at the unannounced interruption. Ready to apologize for the intrusion, Kathleen's eyes darted to the other man's back. Something familiar about his posture, the tweed jacket, caused an elusive memory to flicker though her mind.

The visitor turned around slowly and his gaze met Kathleen's. She fell back against the door, needing the sturdy wood for support. This could not be happening, she told herself. She had crossed an ocean to put distance between the chaos this man had wrought. It was impossible to believe that he was here. It had to be an apparition.

"Hello, Kathleen." Brian's voice was real enough.

"I . . . I . . ." What could she say? Stunned and confused, she said nothing.

"I understand you and Mr. Thomas worked together at Harris and Forbes," Connor said.

"Harris and Forbes, yes . . ." This was madness. How could Brian be standing there, acting civilized when he had turned her life upside down? His broad boyish grin produced an aura of innocence and trust, but she knew better.

"Hello, Brian." Kathleen's voice sounded steadier. She moved away from the door and extended her hand to shake his outstretched one. It was like sleepwalking. She was going through familiar motions like a robot, yet she was apart from it, as though she were disembodied, viewing from outside of herself what was transpiring inside the room.

"I was telling Connor, that I was surprised that you left Harris and Forbes. Everyone knew that you were next in line for department head," Brian said smoothly. "You must have made her a handsome offer, Connor."

As if he didn't know exactly why she left Harris and Forbes! What was he up to? Did he think he could follow her across the sea to try and woo her back? Did he dare to think she was so gullible that he could spin a colorful yarn to block out her knowledge of his part in the company's downfall? Despite John Forbes' generous assessment of Brian's miscalculations, she suspected her ex-boyfriend was a swindler. Otherwise, why the vanishing act?

"I met Brian on my trip to California; he's going to assist us in acquiring a line of china. I must admit, I'm impressed with the legwork he's done. You Harris and Forbes people work fast."

Kathleen searched Connor's face for a clue that he was trying to trick her by bringing Brian here, discredit her, but his amber eyes held no hint of duplicity. Connor O'Shea was unaware of her ex-boyfriend's reputation at home. She had to think of a way to alert Connor to Brian's dealings without sounded vengeful.

Nothing could be accomplished with Brian present. She nearly strangled on anger. What right did he have to appear so appallingly self-confident? He had toyed with several people's careers but seemed to have bounced back from the fray himself.

"I'm calling a meeting this afternoon to apprise everyone of Brian's work on our behalf. If he can speed up a china acquisition, it will put us that much closer to our expansion goals."

"I'd better get back to my office so I can finish my work before the meeting. Goodbye, Brian."

She wished it was truly goodbye, but she knew with a dread that she could not push him out of her life. Brian would leave in his own good time and not before.

"It was good seeing you again, Kathleen." Brian's voice sounded sincere, making Kathleen's stomach turn. She knew he was two-faced, yet she had to be polite and pretend there was nothing untoward in their relationship.

She wanted to be out of there. Cowardly, perhaps, but she had reached her maximum stress level.

She closed the door behind her. Brian's presence posed a threat. If he misrepresented himself with Connor it would cast doubt on her, since he had already alluded to their working together. What else had he told Connor? Would she never be rid of the specter of suspicion her prior relationship with this man created? Not even an ocean could separate his tenacious grip.

She walked to her office, dismayed by the new twist in her affairs. It was almost unbelievable that Connor and Brian could be associated, but the china and glass industry was a tight circle. Everyone seemed to have connections with everyone else. Had Brian known she had been hired by Shea Crystal? Had he contacted Connor because he thought he could trade on her connection with him? Or was this fiasco a coincidence?

Kathleen's nerves were too jangled to concentrate on the crystal arranged on her desk. She doodled across the pad but nothing creative flowed from mind to pencil. There were too many unanswered questions about Brian's untimely appearance.

She flung the pencil to the floor but immediately regretted the childish act. She picked up the broken stub and tossed it into the wastebasket.

The morning dragged. Every piece of copy she had written would have to be torn apart and revised. It was disquieting to have her ability shredded like an old rag by Brian's reentry into her life. Well, if not her life, into the space she was moving in.

She decided to go to the house for a quick lunch before Connor's meeting. Theresa would probably have a sandwich sent over for the sake of conserving time, but Kathleen needed to walk. Her stride was brisk, an attempt to wear herself out and anesthetize her nerves.

Jennie fixed a sandwich plate and Kathleen sat in the alcove and observed the sea while she ate. It helped soothe her, but it would take more than a beautiful scene to create tranquility. *Will I ever experience inner peace again?* she wondered.

Knowing she could not put off returning to the glassworks if she were to be on time for the meeting, she carried her plate into the kitchen, rinsed it and left.

She crossed the parking lot as Brian emerged from the factory. An urge to flee quickened her step.

"Wait, Kathleen! I want to talk to you. Won't you give me a chance to explain?"

The pleading in his voice caught her off guard. She waited for him to catch up and was surprised by the expression of defeat on his face. His mouth tugged downward. His composure was not the earlier, self-assured Brian Thomas. He looked like a child who had just been chastised.

"I know we're through, and I don't blame you. I just want you to know that I never meant to hurt you. I believed the deal I was working on for Harris and Forbes would be successful. It would have put the company in a strategic position. Then negotiations fell through. I'd already sunk all the preliminary investment money into the project. I was in so deep I couldn't see a way out."

"Why didn't you go to John Forbes instead of pulling a disappearing act? Why didn't you let me know things had gone sour? I gave you my savings, Brian. All of it. Surely you owed me an explanation.

"Do you have any idea what it was like at Harris and Forbes after you quit? Everyone blamed me for your problems. I became a freak, Brian's ex-girlfriend, a co-conspirator. Suspicions ran high, and I was the only one left to point to. I know that John Forbes doesn't hold a grudge toward you, but I do."

"Let me finish explaining. Please, Kathleen, hear me out. I met Connor O'Shea in San Francisco and I heard he was in the market for a china line. I thought if I could negotiate a satisfactory alliance for him, the commission might be enough to repay my debts. I've let down a lot of people and I want to make things right. Money can never repay John Forbes for what I put him through, but if I can make some kind of restitution, I'll sleep better at night.

"I know you think I'm a heel, and I don't blame you for feeling that way. But give me another chance. I want to do what is right."

Sympathy welled in Kathleen. She tried to put it aside, but she had known Brian for a long time, and it was hard not to feel some concern for him. Perhaps he was telling the truth about making good on his bad debts. She wanted to believe him and the look in his eyes begged her to accept his word.

"If you tell Connor about my financial problems it will destroy this opportunity. If he doubts my honesty, he'll cancel our agreement. Please don't take this chance away from me. I didn't set out to rip off Harris and Forbes. You know how fickle business can be. The papers were ready to sign but at the last minute Gratton Brothers had one of their loans called in. They downsized their payroll and couldn't guarantee production schedules. Deals go down the tubes all the time. I should have been able to face that, but I had borrowed from you, too, and my ego was shot. Rather than face you, I walked away."

He took her hand. "It was wrong and I'm sorry. Forgive me?"

What could she say? "I don't know. I don't want my position jeopardized. Promise you won't take any risks with Connor's money and I won't interfere."

"I knew I could count on you. You won't regret it." Brian's mouth brushed her cheek. "I wish we could patch things up, Kathleen," he said softly.

That was the last thing she wanted, and she did not want him to harbor any such thoughts.

"No, Brian, it's over. I've got to get back to work." She turned and hurried away. There was nothing more to discuss.

Brian called after her but she did not answer. She caught sight of a movement at an upper window.

The curtain fluttered as though someone had pulled it aside to look out.

She took the stairs to Connor's office at a near run and found herself out of breath. She waited until her pulse slowed before entering the room.

Connor didn't say anything to her—he didn't have to. He brought his wrist up and took an exaggerated look at his watch. He made his point: She was late. Sean drummed his fingers on the desktop, Theresa stared at her notebook. Kathleen privately vowed to be ten minutes early next time.

Connor began the meeting with an update on his attempt to locate a line of china. He told them he had paid Brian a retainer to negotiate acquisition.

Kathleen toyed with her pen, doodling on her note pad. She hated to speculate on how much money Brian had received and whether or not he would be conservative in distributing it. Had he learned anything from the Harris and Forbes fiasco? If he made the right decisions this time, Shea Crystal would benefit. But what if he messed up again? She didn't want to think about the consequences.

She wanted to trust Brian, but was tormented by the fear that he might take advantage of Connor. She cared about the O'Sheas, cared about the glassworks. More than mere employee loyalty, her concern was personal.

The scuffling of chairs jogged Kathleen into realizing the meeting had ended. She hadn't heard a single word Connor had said after the announcement about Brian!

Connor stepped closer to her and said, "That business dinner has been changed to tonight; we'll leave at seven. I've been informed that everyone wants to meet my bright new advertising person."

Was there a note of sarcasm in his voice? Or was she being too sensitive?

She could not shake the unsettling feeling that Brian's visit had upset the delicate balance between her and Connor. Last night they had reached a middle ground. More than a truce, Connor had shown respect for her abilities.

Was that newfound friendship so tenuous that a figure from the past could undo it?

Chapter Eight

The meeting was taking place at Ashford Castle. After some preliminary anxiety about what to wear for such an occasion, Theresa assured Kathleen that the ancient fortress was now a popular inn and she need not fear encountering royalty.

Kathleen drew her hair into a chignon so that she looked, if not stately, respectful of the fact that she would be dining where gentry once reined, and heads of state still visited.

As she dressed, she thought about Connor. She had little patience with his mood swings, but it was best to put aside her irritation and concentrate on this evening's meeting.

She pulled on a mist-green dress that complemented her flame-colored hair. If she were called upon to attend many special dinners, she would run out of dressy clothes. *Worry about that problem when you come to it*, she thought, remembering her fifth-grade teacher's credo: "Never trouble trouble until trouble troubles you."

Well, she had not actively courted disaster but it certainly pursued her lately.

A tap on the door abruptly brought her back to the present.

"Are you ready?"

It was Connor!

She opened the door and he leaned against the doorframe, studying her.

"You look like you're inspecting a piece of Shea Crystal." Her words were brittle.

"Ahh, Kathleen, I'll be the envy of every man at the meeting tonight."

She couldn't tell if he was being sarcastic or complimentary. *Stop being so sensitive,* she chided herself. Connor would not have invited her to this dinner meeting if he didn't want her to go.

Last night, she had been convinced that the turnaround in his behavior was genuine. Why doubt motives now?

She picked up her purse and avoided eye contact with Connor. She knew if their gazes met, he would perceive her insecurity and she wasn't ready to share the questions that were popping in and out of her mind. She didn't want to risk finding out the answers. Perhaps, by the end of the evening, she might have a clue as to where they stood.

"Ashford Castle is in Cong," Connor said, as they got into the Volvo. "A John Wayne movie, 'The Quiet Man,' was filmed there many years ago. The villagers are extremely proud of that and I'm sure a few of my associates will mention it tonight. I hope you've seen the movie so you can act suitably impressed."

She nodded, thankful for the classic movie channel on cable. Connor smiled. Encouraged, Kathleen relaxed. Anxiety slipped away and was replaced by anticipation of an enjoyable evening.

"This is an important meeting. Many of my colleagues would like to expand but they don't have the finances necessary for such a move. It would be a boon to the area's economy if we could provide more jobs. I'm going to suggest forming a cooperative. We could share the costs of an advertising scheme, provide a clerical pool and utilize a central warehouse. Dividing expenses would allow everyone to participate, no matter how limited their resources."

"That's an excellent concept."

"Yes, but it won't be easy drawing my friends away from the old and familiar. They have an inborn resistance to change."

Thoughts of Connor's own resistance to change—to having her work for his company—were on

Kathleen's mind, but she held her tongue. No need to stir up old wounds.

Reaching the village of Cong, they drove along a twisted road that skirted a high stone wall. The wrought-iron gates at the entrance to Ashford Castle were pulled aside and they entered the estate.

A copse of young trees pressed against the roadway and Kathleen could imagine deer taking refuge. Emerging from the sheltering forest, Ashford Castle came into view. The silhouette of the grey stone Georgian was formidable in the waning sunlight. On the highest battlement, a pair of flags, Irish and American, fluttered in the breeze.

They crossed a bridge that spanned a narrow, moat-like waterway. An open touring boat was moored alongside a small dock.

Connor parked the car and turned his attention on Kathleen, his eyes clouding.

"It took years before my sister was accepted by this group. It's not customary for a woman to embrace certain professions. Take it slow. Don't think that because you are determined to prove that you are equal to any man in the business that you can change the mindset of all of Ireland.

"My people are enmeshed in tradition; sometimes they are stubborn. A few of them still refuse to accept Theresa as a peer. I don't want you to be hurt . . . give my friends time to get to know you and most of them will come around."

"Thanks for being candid. I've faced this type of thing before but it's different when you are on home territory. As long as I can count on you to back me up, I'll be all right."

They got out of the car and Connor put his hand on Kathleen's elbow, guiding her up the steps to the entry. He hesitated before opening the door and placed both hands on her shoulders. He didn't speak, but he gazed at her with an expression that was unreadable. His amber eyes were intense. For an instant she felt as though all of the energy was being sucked out of her body. Her knees felt rubbery. Something was going on here, and she had no idea what it was.

He leaned closer, and for a moment she half-expected to be kissed. She shook her head, confused.

Heavy footsteps halted the interplay.

"Evening, Connor," a male voice called.

Kathleen was relieved by the interruption.

"Evening, John," Connor replied. He opened the heavy door and signaled Kathleen to precede him inside.

Kathleen heard muted conversations flowing from the inner recesses of the castle. A woman dressed in a navy skirt and white blouse, obviously the concierge, emerged from a darkly paneled hallway.

"Evening, Mr. O'Shea. The others are having pre-dinner drinks inside."

They entered a spacious drawing room. Tall, velvet-draped windows framed formal gardens and the loch beyond. Diffused light spilled from elegant crystal chandeliers. Connor took Kathleen's arm, guiding her to a group of men, and introduced her.

"So, you're Connor's secret weapon from the United States," one man said.

"We were afraid you were going to keep her under wraps forever," another said.

"I wish I had such a beauty working on my books. Wherever did you find her, Connor?"

"If I revealed that, John, we wouldn't be able to stop the exodus to America."

Kathleen enjoyed the light-hearted banter, especially since it seemed to put Connor into good humor. She was pleased that Connor's earlier warning that his associates might be cool to her had been for naught. They seemed genuinely interested in her.

A few minutes later, the woman who had met them at the door announced that dinner was being served. They entered a large dining room filled with small tables set with starched white linens and glistening china and crystal.

When the meal was finished, Connor broached the subject of a cooperative. He fielded questions, but an obvious skepticism prevailed.

When he returned to their table, Kathleen was

aware of his bristling impatience. He was obviously disappointed that he had not convinced his associates that a united front would be beneficial to trade expansion.

"Connor," she said quietly, "you presented your case well. I'm sure the others will come around. As you said, they are reluctant to let go of old habits. Give them a chance to digest what you told them."

"You're right, but there isn't that much time. It's of the utmost importance to ready our selling campaign for the Christmas season. If the association tries to develop overseas trade, they must enter it well in advance to make up for the delay in surface mail shipments."

"I hadn't thought of that."

John Whelan approached. "Sorry, laddy, if some of these oldtimers don't seem enthusiastic. Your idea is splendid and I've talked to a few of the boys about getting together for a second go-around next week. Given seven days to think about the advantages without listening to someone else's gripes should provide a healthier outlook. We'll meet at my place."

"Thanks, Johnny, I'm grateful to you."

"It's you we should be thanking, Connor. You'll set us back on the road to prosperity, I'm thinking. And that means jobs. Jobs for our young people as well as paychecks for the oldtimers. I'm as fearful of change as any of them, but I know we're doomed without it."

Kathleen liked John Whelan. He was gutsy.

"And bring Kathleen with you to the meeting, Connor. She can soften up the old boys." He laughed and Kathleen could not take offense. She glanced at Connor, and was relieved to see that the laugh lines around his eyes were wrinkled and his mouth curved into a smile.

"She does add a bit of sparkle to the occasion, John, I'll grant you that. And she may even have a bright suggestion or two to contribute."

They left the meeting and Kathleen's thoughts were filled with the details of the evening. Ashford Castle was impressive, even without the fame of a John Wayne movie. And no one had treated her with distance. Connor must be pleased; she certainly was.

She talked nearly non-stop, her enthusiasm like a dam that had burst—it was impossible to stem the flow. It wasn't until they reached Land's End that she realized the conversation had been entirely one-sided. Had she been so wrapped up in herself that she hadn't given Connor a chance to participate, or was something bothering him?

Connor parked and got out of the car. He was at Kathleen's door before she could unlock it. He tugged at the handle impatiently, until she released the lock. Yes, something was needling him and she had the disquieting feeling that it was more than the poor reception to his idea for a cooperative.

"Connor? What's wrong?"

"I saw the way the men looked at you tonight. You're an attractive woman, Kathleen, there is no denying that. I'm wondering if you will be too much of a distraction. Johnny never would have suggested Theresa 'soften up the boys.' But then, Theresa knows her place—she wouldn't flirt with every man in the room."

She struggled to hold back her anger. There was definitely a culture gap at play and she fought against taking his words as a personal affront. This was not the United States, she reminded herself. Misinterpretations were not uncommon, especially in a male-dominated field. And particularly in such a tight circle.

"You told me you wanted your friends to like me. I'm naturally outgoing; accusing me of flirting is an insult."

"Sometimes I think you are the snake in paradise, inviting a taste of forbidden fruit."

"You don't mean that."

"I don't know what I mean. I only know that ever since you arrived I haven't known a peaceful moment."

Without warning, Connor's mouth came down on hers. It was the kiss she had wanted so badly last night. Without thinking, she returned the kiss. Every sensible thought should have sent out warning signals, but the attraction that drew her to Connor was too great. How could she not respond? Connor's arm tightened around her and drew her close against him. She could feel every line of his body meet hers, and his stepped-up heartbeat matched the rhythm of the pounding in her breast.

His kiss would only temporarily blot out their misunderstandings, but she was willing to settle for that. Tomorrow they could hash out problems—tonight she only wanted to be lost in the excitement of their embrace.

Connor's fingers slipped into her hair and he slowly removed each clip from her chignon, dropping them into his jacket pocket. His hands combed the copper strands and became tangled in them as he urged the thick fall into a shimmering cascade across her shoulders.

"That's better," he said. "It's sinful to hide this beautiful hair in a bun."

He cradled her face in his hands and her cheeks became heated by his touch. If he said another word or kissed her again, her bones would turn to mush, she thought.

"You come on pretty strong sometimes, but I guess that's to be expected from an American."

"What do you mean?" She pushed away, startled by the unexpected reversal. "I don't come on to people and Americans don't act any differently than anyone else."

"What about Brian Thomas? I saw that touching scene in the parking lot before he left."

"You were spying!"

"Don't be melodramatic. Or have you been keeping something from me? Something I should know?"

Did he suspect that she and Brian had been close? Even if he had an inkling, he was acting too high-handed for her to allow him the satisfaction of confirming that he was right. Besides, her previous relationship with Brian had nothing to do with her ability to carry out her work at Shea Crystal.

"Brian's an old friend. I wished him well. There's nothing unusual about that."

"That's all?"

If he was testing her, she had boxed herself into a corner. Connor may have misinterpreted the goodbye scene with Brian, but she was not going to explain further.

"I'm going inside, Connor. It's foolish to stand out here in the cold night air and argue."

She shrugged out of his grip and pulled at the door. It was unlocked and she went inside. Connor did not follow and she knew he was brooding. He didn't need company to sulk.

Kathleen stomped up the stairs, and then remembering Theresa, she began to tiptoe.

Inside her room, she closed the door and waited for the sound of Connor's footsteps. When they stopped outside her door, her heart began to pound wildly. She wanted him to come in, to kiss away the anger that had ruined the evening. Yet the sensible side of her insisted that it was better that he walk on. Nothing would be accomplished while tempers seethed.

The footsteps continued on. Relief should have filled her, but instead, Kathleen was hit with a wave of emptiness.

Chapter Nine

Kathleen galloped Baron across a desolate stretch of beach. Behind her, the sky was a mass of storm clouds, but she could see a shaft of sunlight up ahead. She leaned close to the horse's neck, her knees pressed tightly against his sides. Suddenly, a boulder rolled into their path. The stallion reared, then crowhopped into the surf.

Kathleen pitched forward over the horse's withers and into the water. Waves crested and broke and she tumbled underwater. Deep, the water was deep and she was sinking. Down, down, down. Kathleen's feet hit the rocky bottom and she pushed off. She sliced through the water's surface and struggled for a breath of air. If only she could swim to shore. But her arms were heavy, too heavy to move. And she was tired, oh, so tired. Going down again, down. Before the murky water claimed her, she heard laughter, hostile, loud—familiar. Brian's laughter? Or was it Connor O'Shea?

Kathleen bolted upright in bed. Blanketed in semi-darkness, she was momentarily disoriented. Perspiration clustered on her forehead, and her pulse raced. She reached for the nightstand lamp and switched it on.

The light chased the ghosts back into their hiding places. It was a dream. Nothing more. But the message was clear. Her loyalties were at war, and if she was not careful she would be the loser in this battle. She had to set the record straight.

But how much should she explain? She did not want to destroy Brian's opportunity to work with Shea Crystal. It had taken guts for Brian to pursue what he believed was his only chance to make good on his debts.

Perhaps the personal grief he had inflicted upon her had prejudiced her assessment of his failings, placing blame where it did not belong. If John Forbes could be open-minded about Brian, did she have the right to be judgmental? You did not have to be a crook to fail in business. It happened to some of the finest people. Every day.

She would tell Connor about Brian's previous role in her life, and the fiasco at Harris and Forbes.

Surely, Connor would understand. Or would he? It was a risk, but one she must take.

Downstairs, Kathleen met Theresa in the breakfast room.

"You're early, Kathleen," Theresa said.

"I wanted to have a few words with your brother before work."

"Connor left already. He had an appointment in Roscommon. Can I be of any help?"

"Thanks, Theresa, it can wait."

So, the problem would rest between them one more day. And tomorrow? Would she have the same determination to undo the misunderstanding? Or the opportunity?

Later, in her office, Kathleen worked on the catalog.

She grouped a place setting of Thistledown glasses and a decanter on a swatch of black velvet and studied the pieces from various angles. She picked up a water goblet and pressed her fingertips into the grooves, acquainting herself with the aesthetics of the design.

Quick, deft sketches began to flow from her pencil. She loved to draw, and had once envisioned herself an artist. Another Andrew Wyeth, perhaps, or more free in style, like Van Gogh. But it had been commercial art that put bread on the table, and copywriting that furnished the meat and potatoes.

She couldn't complain. Few artists were gifted enough to make it, and she loved her work.

At eleven, Theresa came into Kathleen's office.

"I have to take an order into Westport. Would you like to go with me? We could have lunch."

Kathleen surveyed the mass of papers spread across her desk. She disliked interrupting her work while her creative energy was high, but she sensed that Theresa wanted company.

"I'd love to go, as long as we're back in time for me to finish this layout."

"I promise not to kidnap you for more than a few hours. One of our customers received a large order for our crystal and he doesn't have that much in stock. A sale this size could take care of his rent for six months."

After they delivered the crystal to the Westport shopkeeper, Kathleen and Theresa walked along the town square. They stopped at a modest-looking cafe, and Theresa chose a table near the window. They ordered and when the food was served, Theresa idly toyed with it.

"Is anything wrong, Theresa?"

"I . . . it's Sean. I'm worried about our future. He wants a home of his own, children, a wife to greet him when he returns from the job. There's still so much to do at the glassworks, I can't promise when I'll be ready to offer him those comforts. I sense his impatience, but I can't ignore my duty toward Connor and Shea Crystal."

"What do you truly want, Theresa?" Kathleen spoke softly, touching Theresa's hand, prompting her to respond.

"I'm tired, Kathleen. I simply wish to become Sean's wife and hear secondhand how well Shea Crystal is doing. I'm not a career woman. My position in the company is no longer challenging—it is outright tedious."

"Have you discussed this with Connor?"

"Heavens, no! He would insist I leave Shea Crystal, and marry Sean. But you know how hard Connor drives himself. Can you imagine what it would be like if he took on all responsibility alone? He would kill himself."

"Surely he can hire someone to take your place."

"Connor may be innovative in marketing techniques, but he is tied to tradition. He cannot envision any but family holding the power positions at Shea Crystal.

"My relationship with Sean is doomed. Soon he will look for another woman . . . and there are many on Achill Island who would be happy to have him."

"If you and Sean care for one another, you mustn't give him up."

"Fifteen years from now the women I know will be attending their children's graduation ceremonies at Gortner Abbey and I will still be rushing across the island to deliver a last-minute order to some tiny shop on the outskirts of Mayo." Theresa brushed a tear from her cheek with her knuckles.

The anguish in the woman's voice stilled Kathleen's reply. She didn't know the O'Sheas or Sean Murphy well enough to know who had cornered Theresa into this predicament. Kathleen was an outsider and had no right to offer an opinion, but surely there was room for marriage in this woman's future. How could she love Sean and be willing to give up sharing his life? If family loyalty meant shunning love it was a perverted attribute.

Theresa's expression changed abruptly. "There's Connor!" She stood and tapped the window.

Connor entered the lunchroom with an attractive woman. He took the woman's elbow and steered her toward. Kathleen and Theresa.

"Hello. Don't tell me: Reilly called and needed delivery immediately."

"Yes." Theresa laughed, evidently sharing a private joke. "Arlene, I'd like you to meet Kathleen Flaherty, our new advertising person. Arlene Healy is a buyer for a Grafton Street department store."

"How nice to meet you," Kathleen said.

"I understand you were hired to revolutionize Shea Crystal's catalog."

"It hasn't been put in quite those terms," Kathleen said.

"Knowing Connor, I'm sure nothing less will do," Arlene said, shaking her head knowingly.

"I'm going to show Arlene the ship's decanter we've added to Thistledown. Perhaps it will influence her to increase her summer order," Connor said.

Arlene's laugh was like miniature bells, matching her delicate frame and features.

"Connor never has any trouble talking me into expanding our order. We all know he's a master of persuasion." Her gaze met Kathleen's and a smile curved the corners of her mouth.

Kathleen felt her face become warm and hoped it was not coloring. She knew she was being overly sensitive to suspect that the remark had been directed at her, but the memory of Connor's kiss was too fresh.

"I've got to catch a train," Arlene said, patting Connor's arm.

"You must stop at Brighton's when you're in Dublin," she said to Kathleen. "We carry more than crystal. And we take credit cards." She laughed. "Americans and their plastic, we love them."

Kathleen had no reply. Was Arlene trying to be cute? Or did she view Americans with the "shop till they drop" mentality? If so, she had chosen the wrong person to stereotype.

Connor's expression was unreadable. He looked at his watch, and reminded Arlene that she had a schedule to meet. Kathleen was relieved to see them leave.

"Arlene's a darling. She has been doing business with us for the past five years. Her company's orders have increased each year since she took over the account."

Although she detested petty jealousy, Kathleen could not help wondering if Connor's relationship with Arlene transcended business. Had they been—or worse yet, were they still—lovers? The easy familiarity Connor and Arlene Healy shared was disquieting.

Theresa looked at her watch. "As much as I'd like to prolong this noon holiday, we should return to work."

They drove back to Shea Crystal, each consumed by her own private doubts.

When she returned to her office, Kathleen focused her attention on Thistledown. At the computer she played with arranging shapes of varying sizes across the page and blocked out several spaces for copy she had already put into rough draft. She studied the page, rearranged and studied again until satisfied with the aesthetics. Then she began to shape the copy into final draft.

When the quitting whistle blew she remained at her desk. An hour later, she put her material aside and stood to stretch her cramped shoulders. It was a pleasant exhaustion; she was confident about the copy and layout.

A sour note in the organizational level at Shea Crystal was the reluctance to work with computers. Kathleen's programs were timesavers, but there were more sophisticated programs available to expedite and increase production. Sean had told her that Connor had been difficult about purchasing the printer until Theresa pointed out that it didn't cost much more than an electric typewriter. Perhaps he preferred she write with a quill.

She sat down again. She would polish the copy and then call it a day. Her fingers were flying across the keyboard when the door opened.

"Theresa suggested I look in and see if you were still here. She thought you might be making up for the long lunch." Connor shook his head. "My sister didn't consider that noon interlude business and I see that you don't either. Jennie will be upset if all three of us are late for dinner."

"I'm almost finished."

Connor came to stand behind her so that he could read over her shoulder. It was disconcerting and Kathleen wished he would back off, but there was no way to suggest it without sounding childish.

Connor put a hand on her shoulder and bent closer, his breath a warm moist whisper across her ear. She did not think he was aware that he was too close. Her fingers were suspended inches above the keyboard, frozen, unable to move. She was thankful that he was oblivious to the effect he had on her.

"Go on, don't let me hold you back," he said. "This is good material. No wonder you wanted to stay and finish. I like the presentation. You have really captured the essence of Thistledown. I'm placing bets on this pattern. We hadn't had anything new in our catalog for years; we did well with the old patterns. Since the introduction of Thistledown six months ago, we have had a sizable increase in sales. This has become our top seller."

"A new pattern creates excitement," Kathleen said. "Stores are willing to put advertising dollars into presenting a fresh product.

"The layout is over there." She angled her head toward the corner of the desk, hoping that Connor would move away. She didn't have much luck.

He picked up the paper and sat on the edge of her desk while he studied the sketches. Kathleen hit the wrong key, backspaced, typed, made another mistake, backspaced, and then gave up.

"I'll finish tomorrow." Exasperated, she turned off the computer.

Connor slid off the desktop and stood so close their bodies nearly touched. "This is good, really good. If the rest of the catalog goes as well we'll have a sure winner for our first marketing experience in the States."

She had scored a point! At least in the line of

duty. *And wasn't that the most important thing?* she asked herself. When she accepted the job and Connor had treated her so shabbily, she had promised herself that she would prove him wrong. Why wasn't she exhilarated at receiving his approval?

Because their personal relationship was beginning to become more important to her than their business association. She wanted reassurance in that quarter before he pinned a merit badge on her for a job well done. As a newcomer, she was envious of the women who had a history with him and shared his love of country, his Irish roots, and perhaps more.

Connor's hand rested on her shoulder again. "I'm glad you're on our team," he said.

"Dinner . . ." she reminded him. One more compliment and she would crumble.

When Kathleen reached her room, exhaustion threatened to overcome her. Disrupted sleep and the tension of working on the sketches had taken a toll. She hoped a shower would invigorate her, but knew the laconic drizzle would merely be vaguely refreshing.

A short time later, Kathleen stepped out of the shower. She reached for a towel and wrapped it around her body. She opened the door to the bedroom and stopped short.

"Connor!"

She pulled the towel around herself more tightly,

wishing she had taken time to grab a larger bath sheet from the linen closet. Connor was sitting on the velvet chaise lounge, an amused expression on his face. His laughter made it obvious that he enjoyed the situation.

"I didn't realize . . . but don't look so tragic, Kathleen, you haven't been compromised. I came to see if you had time to join me in a drink before dinner. We could talk a bit more about the catalog."

Connor laughed again. This time it was as though at a private joke. "You didn't think? Kathleen Flaherty, surely you know I'm a gentleman."

A glint in his amber eyes suggested that she did not know anything of the sort.

Chapter Ten

During the following weeks, work went smoothly. Connor showed interest in Kathleen's progress with the catalog, but refrained from criticism. There were occasions when he encouraged her with a compliment on the way she was going about her job. She and Theresa were becoming fast friends, and Sean and Clare were helpful. It was a relief to have pleasant working conditions again, and she settled into the daily routine.

One evening, after dinner, Connor asked Kathleen to follow him into his study.

"I want to show you something. I've been working on an entry for the Presentation Trophy for the Connemara Horse Show. I'd like your opinion."

Connor removed a piece of parchment from a

desk drawer and handed it to her. She sat down to examine a sketch of a horse and rider vaulting a double rail fence. The muscles were shaded, etched lightly, in contrast to the animal's thicker outline. The rider wore formal clothes and was detailed right down to peaked cap and crop.

Kathleen looked up and saw that Connor was gazing at her intently, his eyebrows furrowed; worry lines tugged at the sides of his mouth. Surely he didn't have any doubt about the aesthetics of the drawing?

"It's exquisite, Connor. This would garner all sorts of awards back home. I didn't realize you were so artistic."

"Thank you. It's the first time Shea Crystal has been invited to submit a design. Being a participant is an honor, and winning is not only prestigious, but a financial coup. The winning glassworks cuts the Presentation piece and receives a considerable order for commemorative wine glasses, plus licensing fees for use of the design on shirts and other souvenirs.

"Last year Caven won."

Connor handed her a page clipped from a magazine. It featured a handsome decanter, but the design cut into the crystal did not approach the fine detail of Connor's etching.

"You think I have a chance, then?" It wasn't a question; he was looking for validation.

"You can't miss."

"By the way, has Theresa mentioned the Dublin Home Show?"

Kathleen shook her head.

"It takes place in two weeks. It's a big event; runs Friday to Sunday. We exhibit every year. It's quite an opportunity to put our glass in front of many buyers at one time. The pace is often hectic and we can always use extra representation. Why don't you go with us?"

Go away with him? Could she withstand being so close? Could she keep the business side separate from the personal side? She could not deny the fact that she was drawn to him. He had only kissed her once, but that had sent her into a tailspin. Being together day after day made her even more aware of her desire to turn their relationship into something more. He was obviously attracted to her, too, but he hadn't acted on that attraction since that first kiss.

She knew that a personal relationship with the boss was not wise. She was relieved when the situation did not accelerate, but she could not deny that she ached for more than friendship.

Was this the opportunity? They would be with his associates, his peers. Was an invitation to attend the Dublin Home Show a statement that he was willing to publicly acknowledge her part in Shea Crystal, and perhaps his life? This was his land, his people—was he ready to let her inside?

"Shea Crystal will have a large exhibit. We'll need you, Kathleen."

"Need you." Kathleen turned the words around in her head. She pushed away the obvious meaning, that he needed her professionally. Imagining that he needed her on a personal level brought a shining warmth that would chase away the chill Irish mornings and brighten the darkness of night. She would hope for nothing less.

The following day, Kathleen fiddled with a pencil, idly scribing circles across the writing pad. Connor's invitation to Dublin was racing through her head. She could not shrug off the tension that the images of a weekend with him created, even though the circumstances were business related.

The show was two weeks away. Would her thought processes continue to be disrupted for fourteen whole days? Would she conjure up a romantic scene each day until she had enough to write her own romance novel? How had she gotten into such a predicament? What happened to the "boss is off-limits" code? It had gone out the window with that kiss, she admitted. Business might be business, but none of the rules held up when she was with Connor or thought about him. And she thought about him constantly.

When the noon whistle blew, Clare brought in a tray of sandwiches and tea. Kathleen carried her lunch outside and walked to the edge of the hill for a picnic. It was one of those fine Irish days that called for time outdoors.

A footstep crackled on dry twigs and Kathleen turned to see who was approaching. Sunlight glared into her eyes and she shaded them with a hand. The figure in front of her loomed large and in silhouette.

"Is there enough lunch for two?" Connor's voice emanated from the apparition. Kathleen was momentarily struck silent. It was like seeing a ghost. She had focused on Connor all morning, and now he was at her side. Suddenly, she wasn't sure what was real. Blinking against the sunlight, she watched the tall figure bend, and then Connor was sitting next to her, his long lean frame resting against her, sending a pleasurable ripple along her skin. Their hands touched and Connor's eyebrows arched as his fingertips grazed across her wrist.

"Delicious menu; I may never return to my office."

It was crazy to think that Connor might kiss her, the hill above the ocean was too visible to prying eyes. Someone from the glassworks might see them, anyone driving along the road . . . but his touch, his words hinted that at any moment he might sweep her into his arms. Her imagination was doing wild things, and tendrils of hair at the nape of her neck rose in response.

"I don't know if I can trust myself to be so close to you in Dublin," he said. "It will be hard to resist the temptation to slip into your room when Theresa isn't looking."

Connor smiled. Even though he was teasing, it did not ease the stepped-up beat of her heart or slow the pace of her breathing. If only he knew that she took those very thoughts seriously.

"You know Kathleen, in the old days, this was a fishing village. When the men went to sea, the women left a candle burning in their window to guide them home. If I spy a light in your window, may I take it as an invitation to seek refuge?"

"In California, a candle in the window only means the electricity is out."

"Where's your sense of romance, lass? You've destroyed the mood."

Connor stood and offered his hand to help Kathleen to her feet. They stood close, his breath like the gossamer wingtips of a butterfly fluttering across her cheeks. His hands slid to her waist, then the fingers tightened. A shudder of excitement whipped through her. Was that kiss yet to come?

Connor released her and bent to retrieve the lunch tray. As they walked to the glassworks, Kathleen wondered if he had any idea how much he had disrupted her.

Back in her office, Kathleen worked with sketches and copy, doing cut and paste until, like a puzzle, the pieces fit into an attractive arrangement.

When the quitting whistle blew, Kathleen cleared

her desk. The copy and layout for the Thistledown pattern was complete and she would begin work on the Tawny collection in the morning.

She entered the house and was startled by the sound of a familiar voice wafting through the hall. She hesitated at the base of the staircase before recognition urged her to fly up the stairs. She reached the upper floor in time to escape being seen by Brian and Connor as they walked to the front door.

"I'll contact you as soon as I read the preliminary report on Wellington China," Connor said.

Kathleen heard the front door close as she entered her bedroom. Brian! Back again. And Connor was still ignorant of her previous relationship with him.

Kathleen paced the room. What misguided sense of loyalty had made her believe she owed a measure of allegiance to Brian? He would have to make his own way. She was going to be forthright with Connor and she hoped that her belated openness would not destroy their new relationship.

Perhaps it would be best to wait until after the Dublin Home Show. At least the ties between them would be stronger and better able to survive this predicament.

A knock at the door made her jump. Was it Connor, demanding to know why she had been deceitful? She had not lied, but surely he would view the omission as dishonest.

She opened the door, braced to face whatever

wrath awaited. Connor's expression washed away her anxiety.

"Would you like to go horseback riding before dinner?"

"I'd love it!" She knew her voice sounded too loud, too brittle. In her relief, she would have accepted an invitation to go skinny-dipping in a mud pond with the same enthusiasm.

"Give me a few minutes to change."

Ten minutes later, dressed in denims and sweatshirt, Kathleen hurried to join Connor.

On the way to the pasture Connor told her of Brian's visit.

"Your friend brought me a prospectus on a first-rate china company that is going into receivership. It may be exactly what we need."

"There's something you should know, Connor. While Brian was working for John Forbes he tried to arrange the acquisition of a flatware company. John invested a lot of money in the project. Others invested, too, including me; Brian and I were dating at the time. The buyout fell through, and the money was lost. Rumors started."

"What are you getting at? Do you believe Brian is a fraud?"

"No. I think he's trying to recoup his losses by handling a business deal with you. He claims he'll use his profits to pay back his debtors. That would be great for all concerned. Still, I think you should be aware of his past failure."

"I'll keep it in mind. He seems on the up and up, and he is a go-getter. He's not the first one to have a business deal go sour. I'll give him a chance."

Kathleen was relieved. She didn't want to destroy Brian's chances with Connor, but she had felt obligated to let Connor know the score.

"If Brian comes through with this acquisition before our entry into the American trade, we can include an advertising insert with the crystal catalog. I'll talk to Theresa about it. I'm sure she will have some good ideas."

"You're not planning to dump this on your sister? Theresa is already wrung out from too much responsibility."

"My sister is an extremely capable woman. She's an O'Shea, committed to making Shea Crystal successful. It's a job to you, but it's a way of life for us."

"You aren't being fair. Theresa wants more out of life than a flourishing crystal house. Did it ever occur to you that she and Sean might wish to be married and have a home? You can't tie her to you forever."

A pulse throbbed at Connor's neck. She had struck a nerve, a truth that he did not want to face.

"Theresa needs Sean," Kathleen said softly. "And he wants her. But if she continues to put off marriage, he will begin looking elsewhere. Don't force your sister into years of loneliness. Shea Crystal may fill all the voids in your life, but it's not the same for her."

Connor did not reply. He walked to the lean-to and wrenched a saddle and bridle from a rack and handed it to Kathleen. Without further discussion, they saddled the horses.

Connor stuck his foot in the stirrup and swung into the saddle. His posture was rigid and as he turned to see if Kathleen was ready, his shirt pulled against his chest, showing the rise and fall of his breathing. His agitation was obvious.

Kathleen welcomed a hard ride to wear out their antagonism.

Leaving the enclosure, Connor put his heels to the stallion and the horse broke into a canter. Connor reined the horse so that its gait was slow but smooth. Kathleen's mare responded by breaking into a ragged trot that made her teeth grate. When she kicked the mare in an effort to urge it into a canter, the animal stubbornly continued jogging. Kathleen knew Connor was purposely keeping his horse in check; he was aware that the mare could not match Baron's rocking-horse gait, nor would it pass the stallion.

She could visualize the smug grin on his face: He was punishing her.

She would not allow him to have the upper hand

in this petty game. She reined the mare around and shouted, "Goodbye, Connor!" Confused, the mare crow hopped. Kathleen tightened her leg grip and nudged the mare with her heels and it responded by changing stride.

"That's more like it. No more torture treatment."

Soon she heard the sound of the stallion's hooves pounding the sand behind her.

They galloped across the beach at the tide line, waves splashing the horses' legs. Although the sea air invigorated Kathleen, it was not as stimulating as the athletic motion of Connor's body in front of her.

Connor turned his horse into the meadow and reined it in. Kathleen drew the mare to a halt and the horses nuzzled one another.

"They have the right idea," Connor said. "We might do well to follow their lead." He reached over and looped his hand around Kathleen's neck, pulling her face to meet his. Their kiss was edged with the energy of their earlier anger.

The horses danced closer, their sides meshing against one another. Without warning Connor swept Kathleen off the mare and deposited her sidesaddle in front of him.

"That's better. Anger doesn't suit us."

Kathleen's breath caught in her throat. Blood pumped quickly through her veins and roared in her ears.

The riderless mare grazed on, but the stallion pranced impatiently. Kathleen gripped Connor's shirt, fearful that she would be dislodged from her niche. Connor laughed, his face burrowing into her hair. His hand rested on her thigh and even through the coarse denim she felt an imprint of heat that caused a shudder to careen through her body.

This was crazy! Minutes ago he had thrown angry accusations at her. How could he make such a fast turnaround? The simple statement that "Anger doesn't suit us" wasn't enough to justify the sudden sweetness. She knew that he planned to kiss her again and that kissing him would make it difficult to stand up to him.

Baron continued to prance, tossing his head and yanking the reins from the pommel. The braided leather snaked along the ground.

"Connor!" His name seemed to come from somewhere outside of herself. "The horse . . ."

"Darn," he said gruffly. Connor dismounted and picked up the reins. He stood for a moment, studying Kathleen, his strong, lean body straining against his clothing. She remained on the stallion, needing to gather herself; her heart continued to pound. She pleaded with herself to remain cool, but her body refused to respond.

"Too bad we couldn't have shared another kiss, lass. It would have been interesting to see what developed."

"You're terrible!" she answered. But deep in her heart Kathleen admitted that one more kiss, any time, any place, with Connor would not only be interesting, it would be exquisite.

Chapter Eleven

Kathleen changed into a jersey blouse and skirt and lingered at the dressing table. She gazed at her reflection in the mirror and silently criticized her outfit, her hair, her makeup—or rather, lack of makeup. Was the blue print jersey too loud? Should she have taken time to press the skirt? Did her face look too pale? What about a touch of blush?

She drew the brush through her hair. Still damp from the shower, it stubbornly refused to behave.

Why was she so down on her appearance all of a sudden? She looked fine. *Admit it,* she told herself, *you are delaying, trying to put off going downstairs.*

With good reason. It would be impossible to concentrate on dinner and be politely casual, when all she could think of was how Connor excited her. The romantic entanglement during their afternoon ride made her reassess the decision to go to the Home Show. Granted, it was a professional arrangement, but she was apprehensive about being so close to Connor. Would she look the fool if she backed out? It would be obvious to Connor that she couldn't separate business from . . . pleasure.

Taunted by conflicting feelings, Kathleen went downstairs. Connor was waiting for her in the living room.

"Will you join me in a glass of sherry before dinner?"

"Yes," she answered. Perhaps it would relax her.

They sat on the window seat and observed an approaching storm. Silver gilded clouds floated across a sky swarthed in funereal gray. Mist curled from the damp meadowland and the sea below Land's End churned and boiled like a witch's cauldron.

"It isn't unusual for a squall to hit without warning. Many sailing vessels have been sunk by the violence of a sudden storm. Those rocky inlets are treacherous, and doubly so when gale winds strike."

Kathleen could visualize ships breaking up against the shoals. "And did the widows the sailors left behind still keep a candle burning in the window?"

"Aye, many never gave up hope. Even when the

ship's splinters littered the shore, they fought against believing their loved ones died, until . . . physical proof washed up on the beach. The Irish are known to be loyal and true. It's one of our finest traits."

He took Kathleen's hand. Their gaze met and held and Kathleen wondered if Connor's statement was meant to be a personal declaration.

A flash of lightning cut across the graying light surrounding the meadow. Thunder heralded a torrent of rain. A thick tangle of Scotch broom whipped back and forth in the wind's onslaught. The waves that had peacefully slapped their horses' hooves a few hours ago, now swelled and crashed against rocks and beach.

"The untamed fury of nature is like a love story, don't you think?"

"That's an unusual statement. In what way?"

"The wind is like the bristling excitement of a first meeting, the lightning is the first kiss, and the thunder is the grand pronouncement of love."

"And the rain?"

"Ahh," Connor's head arched back, his eyes closed, "it's the angels' tears of happiness falling on the lovers."

"I never would have suspected that a romantic was hiding beneath that stern countenance. You're a poet, Connor."

"And has my poetry touched your heart?"

Kathleen did not wish to reveal how his images affected her. Not even to herself.

Another flash of lightning sliced through the sky. Kathleen edged closer to Connor. The storm made her nervous. She knew they were safe within the stalwart walls of Land's End, but the scene outside appeared threatening.

"You aren't afraid?"

"Don't be silly . . . well, yes. Yet it's exciting, isn't it?"

"You're exciting, lass. Much more than the storm."

Before Kathleen could answer, Jennie called to them.

"Dinner!"

"Dinner," Connor repeated, winking at Kathleen.

Kathleen felt as though she had just been rescued. But peace did not prevail at the dinner table. Connor's glances were disruptive. Her fork clanked against the water goblet, her napkin fell off her lap, a biscuit rolled off her bread plate. Her clumsiness drew odd looks from Theresa, while Connor was obviously amused by her discomfort.

She wondered how she was going to get through after-dinner drinks without spilling wine all over her clothes. But she need not have worried. When the dessert dishes were cleared, Connor excused himself.

"I'm going to work on the sketches for the Presentation Trophy. I'll join the two of you for a late-night coffee when I'm through."

Kathleen wondered if a respite from Connor's presence would calm her jangled nerves. But even when he was not near her, her thoughts still focused on him. This was a new experience—she had never before found herself so engrossed in a man.

When she dated Brian, he had not filled her thoughts when they were apart. Connor did.

Connor was so completely different from anyone else she knew. He seemed to have separate compartments to his character and personality. One minute he was the hard-driving head of Shea Crystal, the next he appeared sensitive.

"Connor has been working very hard on the Connemara contest," Theresa said.

"Yes, I know. His design is beautiful."

"He showed it to you?"

"Yes. You seem surprised."

"I am. Traditionally, the artist maintains secrecy about his entry. Connor must have been in a most unusual mood to share it with you."

"You mean you haven't seen the sketches?"

"Of course not. The glass cutters believe it is bad luck to allow anyone to be privy to their design before the judging. I would have expected my brother to follow the custom. Did you cast a spell on him, Kathleen?"

Theresa smiled impishly. Kathleen surmised that

the question was half teasing, half serious. And she did not have an answer.

Why *had* Connor shown her the sketches? Kathleen wondered. What prompted him to share a private glimpse of work that was sheltered from everyone else's view? Was it an impetuous move? Connor could hardly be considered impetuous when it came to something as serious as his work. Did it mean that he had taken their kisses as seriously as she had? Dared she hope he was falling in love with her?

Kathleen felt like she was on a teeter-totter. Up and down, up and down. One minute she believed one thing, the next another. Connor was a flirt, and if she read anything more into his attentions, she would court heartbreak.

Ten minutes later, Connor returned and his glance passed over Kathleen, his eyes dark, the lids heavy. A chill of foreboding swept through her when she noticed the furrows on his face, the agitated attention he turned on his sister. His harsh, demanding voice erased the image of gentle poet.

"Theresa, was anyone in my study while I was out?"

"Of course not. What's wrong, Connor?"

"The Connemara entry is missing!"

"My God!" Theresa exclaimed.

Connor and Theresa turned to stare at Kathleen and in that one terrible moment she was afraid they were going to ask if she had stolen it! But that was paranoid, they had no reason to think such a thing. Nevertheless, she suddenly felt like an intruder.

"Did you take it to the glassworks, Connor?" Kathleen asked.

"Of course not. I only worked on it in the security of my study. The curse has come to pass. I never should have shown the design to anyone."

"Surely you don't believe in superstition and old wives' tales?"

"Call it what you will, Kathleen. It doesn't change the fact that my entry disappeared almost immediately after I broke tradition.

"That design stood an excellent chance of winning. I was too complacent; it should have been locked in the vault."

"But who would have thought . . . surely it was safe in the house," Theresa said.

"Can't you work up more sketches?" Kathleen asked.

"There isn't time; we're gearing up for the Dublin Home Show. I'm committed to attending; it's an important event. The deadline for the Connemara competition is the following week. I'm going to look foolish pulling out of the contest at this late date. However, I have no choice."

"I'm sorry, Connor," Theresa said. "You worked so hard. I know that you counted on having your entry in the show book. But you can try again next year."

"If I'm asked. I don't know how they will regard my withdrawal. We needed that contest. With the extra expense of entering the American market, the exposure in the show book would have brought in more orders. The publicity alone is almost as important as winning the prize. And if we won, it would have meant more jobs here on Achill Island. Our young people would not have to run away to the city to get work."

"I'll talk to Jennie," Theresa said. "Perhaps she cleaned the study and put the sketches away."

"The sketches could not be mistaken for clutter, Theresa. Besides, Jennie knows well enough not to tamper with my work."

Theresa left to talk to the housekeeper and Kathleen thought it was an excuse to separate herself from the unpleasant situation. She knew as well as Connor that Jennie had no hand in the missing papers. But who did?

Connor paced; the atmosphere bristled with tension. Kathleen wished she had a reason to excuse herself, not wanting to get caught in the electrical force. But that would be cowardly.

"Theresa told me it was highly unusual to be shown the design before the judging. I was pleased that you had taken me into your confidence. I took it as a sign that we were finally friends. Now I feel somehow to blame, yet that's foolish. I don't believe in hexes, so I can't be responsible."

"Perhaps I'm overreacting. I don't believe in the 'little people' or four-leaf clovers, but that doesn't change things. The design is gone. What other way is there to explain its disappearance? I broke a code that has been observed for generations. I would rather believe in bad luck than chicanery."

"You're not pointing your finger at me, are you?"

"Of course not."

Kathleen did not hear conviction in his answer. Or was she being too sensitive? Emotions were running high. The loss of the sketch was devastating to Connor, no doubt about it.

"I wish I could help in some way; take your mind off this, somehow." She touched his arm, hoping he would realize her concern, but he seemed immune to her caring. Nobody could reach him, Kathleen realized. What had occurred was a tragedy, and only Connor could comprehend the depth of it. He stood alone in his grief. She could feel sorry for him, but she could not identify with his loss. His concern for his countrymen was uppermost, and his vision of additional employment on Achill Island had been dashed.

He turned away from her, insulating himself from being consoled. "I'm going to stay in my study for a while longer, Kathleen. I'm not good company. Why don't we call it a night."

She was being locked out . . . of his mind and his heart.

"Good night," she said softly, and walked quickly out of the room before he could see that tears had pooled in her eyes. Shadows pursued her up the curving staircase.

In her room, she stared out the window at the dwindling storm. Just hours ago, she and Connor had enjoyed flirty remarks as they watched the lightning spark across the rocky hillside. They had shared a closeness. Now he was shutting her out, refusing to discuss what was important to him. It made her feel diminished, unwanted.

Vivid images swirled through her consciousness; memories of being held in Connor's arms, feeling his mouth on hers, the excitement of his newly created sketches. Feeling and sharing; it was all gone with a sweep of a hand, the loss of a sketch.

She didn't blame him for being upset; anyone in his predicament would be. But to push her away, when they were getting so close . . . Kathleen brushed the tears from her cheeks with the back of her hand. Would happiness always elude her?

Stop feeling sorry for yourself, she silently instructed. *You're strong; you can take whatever is handed out.*

It wasn't too late to rescue her twice-bruised self-esteem.

Chapter Twelve

During the days that followed the loss of Connor's sketches, Kathleen worked at her desk relentlessly. Completion of the catalog was nearing and she was happy to be close to her goal.

She and Connor rarely saw each other except occasionally at dinner. He seemed as wrapped up in his work as she was in hers. She missed his company; it was as simple as that. When she was down in the doldrums, she allowed herself to dwell on the possibility that he was purposely avoiding her. Other times she realized that they both had hectic schedules. The only difference was that Connor seemed to thrive on his.

The emptiness his absence created left her with an insatiable yearning. Without him, part of her was missing. If only they could take time out from business and reach out to one another on a personal level. Discuss what was going on. If only he would talk about it, let her inside so that she could understand what he was going through. Business linked them, but it also pushed them apart.

She suspected that he was overcompensating for the loss of the Connemara sketch. As though overextending himself would blot out the memory. It wouldn't work, however, because he had depended on the Connemara entry bringing more attention to the glassworks. He was a man intent on a single goal: bringing Shea Crystal to the top. Being forced to drop out of the Connemara competition was a major blow.

Kathleen strained to focus on the pages in front of her. The first half of the catalog was camera ready and would be displayed at today's staff meeting.

When it was time, she gathered the portfolio and met Theresa in her office.

"I'm anxious to see what you've done with the catalog so far," Theresa said. "Actually, we all are. I thought I would have a chance to stop in your office for a look, but time seems to get away."

"I know."

"I'm grateful that you are going to the Dublin Home Show with Connor," Theresa said, as they walked upstairs to the meeting. "It allows me to spend Sunday in Westport with Sean. I know I must reach a decision about our future. Perhaps being away from Shea Crystal and Land's End will facilitate that."

Kathleen was dazed. "Connor still expects me to go to Dublin with him?"

"Of course. He hasn't said otherwise, has he? Clare made the reservations. I understood that you were going to assist him at the exhibition hall. You haven't changed your mind?" Worry lines edged Theresa's face.

"No, but Connor and I haven't exchanged more than a dozen words this past week. In fact, I have been trying to decide whether he was avoiding me, or if he was overworked. It would have been easier to flip a coin for the answer."

"This is a busy time for Shea Crystal. Connor hardly takes a minute to speak to me, either, except to give orders." Theresa smiled. "He's counting on having you attend the Home Show, and so am I."

"I just don't understand him, Theresa. Sometimes I feel we are close, other times he is so distant."

"He doesn't mean to be enigmatic. It's the business that drives him. It sometimes gets in the way of his personal life. Connor is a good man.

"He cares for you, Kathleen. Don't ever doubt that."

"Thanks for the encouraging words. Now here is a tip for you: Before you make any decisions concerning your future, talk to Connor. I've already spoken to him, so it won't come as a surprise."

"You told Connor? What was his reaction?"

"He accused me of interfering, but I'm sure he thinks differently now that he has had time to reflect on the matter. You've got to impress upon him that you plan to delegate some of your responsibilities immediately so that you can ease out of your position smoothly."

"Connor would never agree . . ."

"No one is indispensable, Theresa. Don't allow your brother to insinuate that the glassworks can't survive without you. Clare can handle personnel. Her experience with public contact provides an excellent transition. Change your policy on emergency deliveries; no one else would offer such service. If a shopkeeper is desperate for a shipment, he can pick it up himself.

"Sean can assist with scheduling. He's in the heart of production and is probably best informed on that score.

"A full-time advertising person can double as buyer-liaison.

"And start computerizing. I'm willing to show you what programs fit your needs and I'll help set up a software training class. When necessary, you can pitch in and telecommute for a couple of hours a day at home."

"You're quite a problem solver, Kathleen. A lot

of thought has gone into this plan. Maybe I *can* abdicate my position without adversely affecting the glassworks."

"No 'maybe's,' Theresa. You must do it!"

"I hope you'll stay on, Kathleen. I know you only agreed to work on this project, but we've come to depend on you for more than developing a new catalog. I can't imagine what it would be like without you. If you remain on the staff, I can leave Shea Crystal without any regrets."

"There is so much to consider. As much as I have grown to love Ireland, I can't make a decision yet."

"You do enjoy your position at Shea Crystal, don't you?"

"Yes, and I'll always be grateful for this opportunity. We'd better hurry; we don't want to keep your brother waiting."

They entered Connor's office. Sean and Connor were talking. Without interrupting, Kathleen placed her portfolio on Connor's desk. He picked it up and thumbed through it while listening to Sean. His eyes were narrowed and for a brief moment Kathleen thought he was going to criticize. It would not be justified; she was confident about her work. This catalog was a winner.

Connor looked up. His attention fastened on Kathleen.

"These are outstanding. I didn't realize you were so far along. Sean, Theresa, take a look at these."

They crowded around Connor's desk and Kathleen studied their expressions as they examined her work. Hungry for approval after such an exhausting week, she was rewarded by Sean's grin and Theresa's wide smile.

"You've certainly proven yourself, Kathleen," Theresa said. "I told you when I found this jewel that you wouldn't be sorry, Connor."

"First rate, lass," Sean said. "I hope you're going to be a permanent fixture hereabouts."

"I . . . I . . ." The compliments were like wine, intoxicating in such a large dose.

"When will you be finished? I'd like to use this as a model for the cooperative's brochure."

"Has the concept been accepted, Connor?"

"Yes. Last night I finished a workup on a management plan and a financial projection. I didn't realize it would involve so much time but it had to be a persuasive package in order to be successful. I made a presentation this morning and we signed the preliminary agreements. If we move quickly, we will be ready for the Christmas buying season."

"That's wonderful."

That was why he had locked himself into his study night after night. Theresa was right, Connor had not been avoiding her.

"The rest of the artwork and copy should be finished in two weeks, Connor. If your associates supply me with photos and price lists, I can do some layouts for the cooperative catalog in my spare time."

"You would do that?"

"I think it's a fantastic project, Connor. It would be exciting to take part in its success."

"The men will especially appreciate having an American give them inside tips on overseas advertising."

Sean caught Kathleen's eye and winked. He obviously enjoyed the turnaround in Connor's attitude. It was easy to remember the first encounter in this room when Connor had tried to cut down her professional ability. They had traveled a long way for Connor to publicly admit a change of heart.

When the meeting was over, Theresa and Kathleen walked downstairs together. Before returning to her office, Theresa said, "I hope the overwhelming appreciation of your work will tip the scales in our favor when you make a decision about remaining at Shea Crystal."

Kathleen smiled. "It's amazing what a few compliments can do to a person's self-esteem. All of a sudden I don't feel like an outsider any more."

"You were never an outsider, Kathleen. I'm not blind, I've seen how my brother looks at you. If he seems ambiguous, it may be because of an old wound. Connor fell in love while he attended Stanford. It was serious. At least on his part. It turned out the young woman he was in love with had a boyfriend back home in Detroit and Connor was only someone to while away the hours until the semester was over. It nearly destroyed him. He has judged all American women by that experience, I'm afraid. I think you're just the person to re-educate him.

"Don't let petty misunderstandings get in the way. Take some of your own advice: Talk to him."

"Theresa, set a good example and marry your Sean!"

"I think I will, Kathleen, and I'll want you to be my maid of honor. Yes, I think Sean and I will set the date this weekend."

Theresa threw her arms around Kathleen and gave her a hug. "Make the most of your trip to Dublin, lass. Understand?"

Kathleen laughed and Connor's sister joined in.

"I will, Theresa, I swear it."

Thursday, remembering Theresa's parting hug, Kathleen smiled to herself. The ride to Dublin had been pleasant. Connor was in an excellent mood, filled with anticipation of the exhibition.

They had reservations at Jury's Hotel and Kathleen waited in the lobby while Connor checked in for them.

A bellhop appeared and captured their luggage, whisked them onto the elevator and led them to their rooms. Kathleen tipped the aging bellhop, and followed his gaze to the door that separated her room from Connor's.

Connor knocked and Kathleen unlocked her side of the door. He waved a bottle of wine.

"Shall we have a glass before we go downstairs? We have reservations for the dinner show; I'm sure you will enjoy it."

Connor poured the wine and they stood by the window viewing the city bustle. A fire-engine red double-decker bus trudged along, vying with bicycles and compact cars for street space. The sidewalk was bordered by umbrella-like trees and concrete bowls spilling masses of white flowers. Dublin. Nearly as busy as San Francisco, yet so very different.

Connor put his drink on the window sill, took Kathleen's glass from her hand, and placed it beside his. The glasses created a bell sound as they touched. Standing behind Kathleen, he put his arms on her shoulders and turned her to face him.

"Do you know how much I've wanted to hold you? It seems like such a long time." His eyes communicated longing, a longing Kathleen shared. She wanted to forget all the insecurities the rift had created.

"Ahh, sweet Kathleen," Connor's mouth moved across hers. "You drive me mad. I'm sorry that I reacted badly about the sketches. Sometimes I lash out without thinking. I have no regrets about showing you the design and I'm not foolish enough to believe in curses. I was frustrated over the loss, nothing more. The contest was important to me, and although I don't understand what happened, I am not going to let my disappointment ruin what we have together."

His mouth met hers again and the heady taste of wine teased her lips. Her heart pounded and she knew that this was a precarious moment. She longed to remain in his arms, to encourage his kiss to last indefinitely, but that would be madness.

"Connor, I have to change for dinner."

She hated to push him away. She wanted to remain in his arms, to be kissed, needed. He was right, it had been a long time. Too long. But her emotions were running high and she did not want to find herself in a predicament that she was unable to handle.

"Connor," she repeated. "Please . . ."

Connor nodded, and without another word, returned to his room. She watched him pull the connecting door shut behind him. Closing the door did not shut out thoughts of their kiss.

Later, they were ushered into Jury's large dining room by the hostess. The decor was elegant. Crystal chandeliers sparkled overhead and white tablecloths created a formal atmosphere. They were led to a table close to the stage. They ordered dinner and had a bottle of champagne brought to their table. The wine steward showed Connor the label on the bottle, and poured a small amount into a glass for Connor's approval.

Minutes later the stage burst into life with lights, music and dancers. An Irish tenor sang traditional ballads. Some Kathleen knew, others she had never heard before. There were sad songs of unrequited and undying love, poignant devotions to Irish mothers, and joyous songs of rainbows and marriage. In between, the show was spiced with jigs and reels.

Jury's shining star, Hal Roach, a Barry Fitzgerald look-alike, had Kathleen laughing until her sides hurt. His satires of the Irish were spiked with humorous mimicry. He had a ready audience, open to laughing at themselves.

The lighthearted atmosphere was a delightful reversal of the weight of the past week. Connor reached across the table and their fingertips touched. "Having a good time?"

"Yes."

"I'm glad. I've been so busy with the cooperative plans, I know I've neglected you. I'll make up for it. This will be a wonderful weekend. There will be time in between Home Show appointments to tour Dublin. You will be amazed at the city's history; it has been the center of turmoil, as well as Irish culture. If Theresa were here she would take you on a shopping binge along Grafton Street."

"Connor, I've been thinking about Sean and Theresa. You know they want to get married. Isn't it time to ease your sister out of the responsibilities she shoulders?"

"Kathleen." His eyes darkened, and a muscle twitched at the side of his cheek. "This is our time together, don't spoil it."

"It's important, Connor. Theresa is spending the weekend in Westport with Sean. She is at a turning point in her life. I know how you feel about the reins of Shea Crystal remaining within the family, but if Theresa and Sean get married, he *will* be family. Don't make it difficult for your sister—help her break free. You won't lose her, she'll always be vitally interested in what course Shea Crystal takes. She loves you so much, Connor, she doesn't want to go against you. Give her the chance to be fulfilled, truly fulfilled."

Connor turned away. Kathleen knew he was wrestling with a brush of anger. Then he turned back to face her. His eyes seemed to gleam with understanding and a smile softened his expression.

"You're right. When we get back, I'll give my sister my blessing."

"You won't be sorry."

"All this talk about love is getting to me." Connor's voice was like velvet.

Kathleen touched a finger to her mouth and then pressed it on Connor's lips. "Will that hold you until we're alone?"

"Lass, that doesn't even qualify as an appetizer."

Connor put some bills on the table and he pulled Kathleen's chair away from the table and she stood. His hand claimed hers, his fingertips teasing the palm as they walked.

"Let's stop at the pub before we retire."

They walked down the street to a small pub. A large wooden sign, *Paddy's*, hung above a brick-front doorway. They entered and Connor indicated a corner table. The place was filled with people dressed in casual clothes, boisterously crowding around the bar. A few well-dressed patrons clustered around small lacquered tables.

"You must try our famous Guinness ale while you're in Dublin." He ordered two half pints and the waitress returned with their glasses.

A small bandstand contained a pair of fiddlers who were frantically playing a medley of jigs to the accompaniment of clapping hands.

When the eleven o'clock curfew was announced, the musicians changed tempo and everyone stood up and began singing in Gaelic. Kathleen stood very still, mesmerized by the scene. No one had to spell out the fact that they were singing their National Anthem. It was suggested in their posture, in the way the men clutched their hats tightly against their hearts. It was an intimate glimpse of the Irish people that Kathleen would always remember.

When they were finished, the bartender told them to drink up.

They walked back to the hotel and took the elevator to their floor. Kathleen was suddenly nervous. Their rooms were only separated by a door, a door that Connor could easily open.

So far, he'd been a gentleman, keeping his emotions in check.

As though sensing her unease, Connor bent and kissed her on the forehead. A brotherly gesture that immediately put her anxiety to rest.

Chapter Thirteen

The bustle of the Home Show kept Kathleen occupied. She had not seen Connor since they set up Shea Crystal's booth. They planned on attending the evening performance of the horse show and she wondered if that would be the only time she would see him all day.

Not that she was bored; tourists and Irish alike stopped to view the crystal and ask questions. Kathleen was glad she had done her homework, especially when confronted with the raised eyebrow accompanying the question of why an American was representing an Irish house. Sometimes she pondered the same question, but with much different answers than those she gave the curious public.

"Hello, Kathleen." A familiar male voice jostled her.

"Brian. What are you doing here?"

Brian leaned across the counter and took her hand. Out of the corner of her eye, Kathleen noticed a shopper observing them. Not wishing to cause a scene, she did not pull away from his grip.

"I'm here to learn about the various home accessories. If I remain in Ireland, I'm going to have to do more than sell a line of china to your boss."

"Brian!"

Connor strode up and, guiltily, Kathleen withdrew her hand, but she knew the contact had not gone unnoticed.

"How is the acquisition coming along?"

"Quite well, Connor, but we're going to need more money to firm up the transaction. Will that present a problem?"

"Not at all, but I thought the advance represented a sizable deposit."

"I would have thought so too. Perhaps Wellington is taking advantage of me because I'm an American."

Connor laughed. "I'll have Theresa draw a check as soon as we return to Land's End. The sooner we tie up this arrangement, the better. If you're staying on, join us for the horse show tonight."

Kathleen silently prayed that Brian would be too busy, but she knew he would accept the invitation.

“I’d like that,” Brian said.

“We’re staying at Jury’s. Why don’t we meet in the lobby at seven-thirty, and go over together.”

All right. See you then.”

“Nice chap.” Connor’s gazed seemed to challenge Kathleen. Or was she reading messages where there were none? Her anxieties obviously colored her perception.

Brian seemed to appear every time she turned around. Not that it was unusual for him to be at the Home Show. After all, he was in the business, too. Still, she wished he hadn’t interrupted the pleasant flow of her day. Brian’s presence made her nervous.

An elderly woman interrupted Kathleen’s musings. The distraction was welcome. No use beating herself up over something she could not readily change.

The woman was dressed in a plain shirt-waisted dress. Despite her simple outfit and her age, her appearance was striking. Her skin was porcelain smooth and clear blue eyes were accented by a royal blue silk paisley scarf artfully draped at the neck.

Although Kathleen thought the woman was merely browsing, it turned out she owned a gift shop in Galway.

“My granddaughter runs the store, now,” she told Kathleen. “I’m semi-retired and combine buying trips with short vacations. When I managed the store I was so busy, I hardly had time to shop for food for the table, much less fancies for the store. Most of our goods came from a catalog.

"My granddaughter is a Trinity graduate. 'Gran,' she told me, 'the shop's gone stale. You have to be progressive to make it nowadays.' She's right, you know. Good businesswoman, my Meggie." She beamed, and Kathleen half-expected her to whip out a snapshot of Meggie and was halfway disappointed when she didn't.

"We have a bridal section now, and Meg told me to be sure to choose some high-class wine glasses at the show. I like the looks of this one." She picked up a Thistledown champagne flute.

"That's a popular pattern, my favorite, too." Kathleen said.

"Do you have a bridal registry, so the bride-to-be can sign up for the gifts she wants?"

"Yes. Another of my granddaughter's ideas. Says it's popular in America. Is that true?"

"Most department stores use registries and it seems to work," Kathleen answered.

"Innovative, Meggie says. Key to drawing new customers and keeping old. Ideas seem to jump out of her head all the time. Can't keep up with her." She leaned over the counter and said softly, "Keeps me young, though." Then she stepped back and laughed.

What a delightful woman, Kathleen thought. How

lucky she and her granddaughter were to have each other.

After a fifteen-minute discussion about patterns and types of wine and water glasses, Kathleen wrote up a sizable order. She promised a two-week delivery date, and hoped that would not present a problem. Connor had neglected to advise her on that aspect of sales.

At five o'clock, Kathleen closed the booth. It took almost an hour to pack the displays and look up before she could return to the hotel.

A hot bath was uppermost in her mind. Kicking off her shoes, she stripped on the way to the bathroom, eager to sink into a tubful of steamy water. She turned on the faucets and sprinkled bath crystals under the running water.

She had been on her feet too long. A soak to soothe her tired body was definitely the prescription. She stepped into the tub. *Ahh, delicious,* she thought, sinking lower into the water. The bubbles patted a lacey shawl around her. It was like a pool of vanilla milkshake.

She closed her eyes, attempting to blot away fatigue, both physical and mental.

Later, dressed in navy slacks and a red and white blouse, she called room service to send up a tray. Connor had told her to eat without him—he had appointments all afternoon. They were to pick up their horse show tickets at the lobby desk and leave at 7:30.

When her hot turkey sandwich arrived, Kathleen was ravenous. *Serves you right for skipping lunch,* she admonished herself. *No time,* her alter ego answered.

The phone rang. Kathleen answered, assuming it was Connor. She was surprised to hear Arlene Healy's voice.

"Connor invited me to join you. I wanted to make sure that didn't interfere with your plans."

"Not at all," Kathleen answered. What else could she say? She had hoped to have Connor all to herself? That might not have been an option, anyway, since Brian probably intended to tag along, too.

"Shall I meet you in the lobby? Connor said seven-thirty. I'm only down the block."

"See you then," Kathleen said.

Brian was waiting when Kathleen arrived downstairs. Arlene Healy showed up a few minutes later, with Connor at her side.

"We ran into each other," she said. Kathleen was amused by Arlene's need to explain.

The arena was a short walk from the hotel. Brian fell into step alongside Arlene, and the hum of their conversation drifted to Kathleen while she and Connor exchanged news of the day. Connor complimented her on wrapping up the sale to the Galway store and assured her that she had given an acceptable delivery date.

Reaching the arena, they were seated a few minutes before the performance started. The horses had been brushed until their coats shone, and the riders were dressed in tweed and cords. Connor was informative. His knowledge of horses and the individual show riders provided a steady flow of information.

Arlene Healy and Brian seemed to have found an instant compatibility and Kathleen thought she had caught them touching hands quite often, but when noticed, Arlene drew apart almost shyly. Was Brian interested in Arlene? It would not surprise her if Arlene was attracted to him: he was good looking and had charisma. Women fell for him; Kathleen was proof of that.

Arlene and Brian's attachment was not her concern. Even though she was beginning to like Arlene and would hate to see her get hurt, she wasn't going to let any touchy-feely games ruin the magic of the Dublin sojourn.

After the horse show, they returned to the hotel and went to the lounge for a nightcap.

They were seated at a small booth and Kathleen was intensely aware of Connor's knee against her leg. Conversation was animated: horses, the Home Show, marketing—Brian's hands in motion to emphasize a point, Connor's eyes darkening as he criticized a competitor's marketing strategy, Arlene's comments on a winter fashion trend that was destined to fail. Kathleen mostly listened, snug in a cocoon of chatter, lulled by congeniality.

Anyone observing the foursome would think they had known each other for years, she thought.

When the talk wound down, Brian lifted his glass.

"I propose a toast: To Ireland, Shea Crystal, and the friendship and success of the four of us."

The glasses tinkled as they met, and Arlene momentarily leaned her head against Brian's shoulder. Kathleen perceived a shift in Connor's posture and attitude, and it left her with a chill. Was her imagination working overtime?

They finished their drinks and got up to leave. Brian offered to walk Arlene to her hotel.

"I'm going to stop by the desk and see if there are any messages for me," Connor said.

Kathleen waited for him in the hallway. He returned a few minutes later and seemed agitated. They stepped onto the elevator.

"What's wrong, Connor?"

"I received a telegram from an associate. I'm going to have to spend a couple of days in Limerick. I'm leaving first thing in the morning. You'll have to see to the exhibit without me. I don't like deserting you but it can't be avoided. Perhaps you can get Theresa to come down and help."

"She's in Westport."

"I said it can't be helped, Kathleen."

"Do you want me to join you when the show is over?"

"No, I'll arrange to have Brian drive you back to Land's End. Finishing the catalog is more important than chasing after me."

She didn't understand the sudden mood swing. If he had received bad news, why didn't he share it with her?

Connor took Kathleen's key from her hand and unlocked her suite. He pushed open the door and stood aside for her to enter. Locking the door after himself, he strode to the connecting doorway between the rooms. He stopped a moment and a distant expression crossed his face. His eyes became hooded and Kathleen could not read them.

"Good night, Kathleen," he said, and abruptly strode into his room.

What had gone wrong? Why had a shadow crept over the sunbeams that had brightened their weekend?

Connor's sudden coldness coincided with the arrival of the telegram. Why hadn't he shared the news, told her what was wrong? The missing element in their relationship was trust. An important element. He always held back a part of himself, and was unable or unwilling to be open with his problems. That tended to put the brakes on their romance. Romance? Kathleen knew that she was more involved than that. She loved Connor. Was she ready to risk another heartbreak to pursue that love?

Kathleen changed into her nightclothes, crawled into bed and slipped under the down comforter.

She felt so alone. On the other side of the wall was a man who possessed the power to light up her life one minute, and plunge it into darkness the next. She was trapped in a need for him that precluded escape.

Chapter Fourteen

Connor had departed from the hotel before Kathleen woke up. He probably left too early to wake her, she reasoned, but still it bothered her not to know what had upset him.

So much for the grand tour of Dublin, Kathleen thought wryly. Her love life was going nowhere; perhaps she should join a nunnery while she was in Ireland and be done with it!

The final day of the Home Show breezed by quickly. Kathleen had to do the work of three people, but she managed. She couldn't take Connor's advice to call Theresa. His sister needed uninterrupted time with Sean.

She was relieved when it was time to pack up and grateful when Brian arrived and assisted. He took over the shipping arrangements while she returned to the hotel to retrieve her suitcase.

When they were finally on the road, she wiggled her feet out of her shoes. Either the leather pumps shrunk during the past few days or her feet were swollen. She wished she had packed her running shoes.

Brian became expansive on the drive to Achill Island, taking Kathleen into his confidence, perhaps encouraged by the acceptance he had received the other night. She was too distracted by thoughts of Connor to pay much attention to her ex-boyfriend's ramblings about his ambition to settle in Ireland. It was talk, nothing more. In another month Brian would probably return to the United States.

"Arlene Healy has excellent connections with the big department stores in Dublin and Cork," Brian said.

Kathleen's head jerked around. Mention of Arlene Healy immediately caught her attention.

"What about Arlene?"

"Arlene can use her connections to help me get established. She offered to introduce me around. It doesn't hurt to have an 'in.' "

"Arlene hardly knows you!" Kathleen protested. "You can't expect her to recommend you. It's unprofessional."

"Don't be naive, Kathleen, it's done every day.

Arlene and I hit it off and she's more than eager to do me a favor."

Brian turned to look at her. "Isn't that how you got your job with Shea Crystal? Did you flash a sweet smile and wide innocent eyes?"

"Are you assuming there must be a questionable motive because you always play the angles? There was nothing personal involved in my coming to Shea Crystal. The Harris and Forbes takeover left me high and dry. John Forbes knew I was looking for a job and he arranged an interview with Connor's sister. She liked my work and offered me the position. It was completely above board. They needed someone to develop a new catalog, I had the qualifications and needed a job. It was a straightforward arrangement."

"With all the unemployment around here, you're going to tell me that you were the only available advertising person? Be real."

"Brian, I don't care what you believe, just don't misrepresent yourself when it might reflect poorly on me."

"Get a hold of yourself, I'm not planning anything shady. Trust me, Kathleen, it's just that I need every break I can get."

"I don't know Brian, sometimes I think you're trying hard to square things and then your off-the-wall remarks make me suspicious. When you sound like you're taking advantage of someone I get nervous. I don't want to rub it in, but the 'help' you gave John Forbes didn't exactly create a business boom. He would probably still be at his desk—and so would I—if your idea hadn't sent the company down the tubes."

Brian reached over and patted her hand. "Same old Kathleen, afraid of taking risks. If I don't grab any opportunity that comes my way, life will pass me by and I'll never get anywhere."

"You were doing pretty well before . . ."

"Don't say it." His hand brushed her lips, a disconcerting gesture.

Kathleen turned to stare out the window again, pushing aside the unsettling thoughts that Brian provoked. She hoped he was being honest with everyone, but something nagged at her. Was it the fact that he had asked Connor for more money? Or was it the way he had become so attentive toward Arlene? Not that the Healy woman wasn't attractive, and she had an engaging personality, but he had come on to her too quickly.

Kathleen suspected that Brian was a user after all, so eager to get what he wanted that it didn't matter how many others he trampled along the way.

She couldn't stand it if Brian was leading Connor into a scam.

"Brian, how much of an advance did Connor give you for the acquisition of this new line of china?"

"You know what curiousity got the cat, Kathleen . . ."

Undaunted, she persisted, "And how much more are you going to ask for to consummate the proposition?"

"Kathleen, you know I can't discuss the financial aspects of this deal. It would be betraying my fiduciary relationship with my client."

"Forget the fancy words, Brian. I want to know how much Connor is into you for."

"Don't worry, your boyfriend will get value for his investment. We'll both benefit. I couldn't ask for better references than being Connor's agent. Doors open magically and without question. The Irish are rather trusting, or is it naive?

"Soon, I'll be able to forget the sordidness that plagued me. I can even forgive you for your lack of loyalty. You'll see, Kathleen, I'm going to do well in Ireland, I've got more investments going than you can imagine."

"You certainly talk a good game, Brian. I know you were broke when I left San Francisco. Does this windfall of investment money have anything to do with Connor?"

Brian didn't answer right away. Kathleen sensed that his eagerness to brag was conflicting with the necessity to be secretive. His ego won out.

"I have put part of the advance to good use while we're waiting for the agreement to be effected. At today's paltry interest rates, it seemed a waste to let it sit idle in a bank account. I consider it a loan against my commission."

"Is that what you did with John Forbes' money? And mine? Is that what got you into trouble before? You're a gambler, Brian, not an investor!"

"Stop worrying. Nothing can go wrong this time."

"I want you to level with Connor."

Brian turned to appraise her. A thin smile darkened his expression.

"I have been level with Connor. It was easy getting his business once he knew of our rather close friendship. To make the story more colorful I told him that I had broken up with you and that I suspected you took this job to get over being jilted."

"Why would you do that?"

"I needed this deal and if I had to trade on our past to get it, so be it."

"Darn you, Brian, if you mess up my life again you will regret it. I'm going to let Connor know that you can be deceitful. You won't get a second cash advance, you can be sure."

"Connor won't believe you, he'll think you're being vindictive."

"I guess I'll have to risk it."

At Land's End, she excused herself from being present at dinner, begging a headache rather than sit across the table from Brian's deceitful face. Connor had invited him to remain at Land's End until his return. How would she maintain her equilibrium during the following days?

She should have been safe from Brian's tricks here in Ireland. After all, an entire ocean had separated them and the upheaval he had wrought. But Brian was slick. He had evidently thought out his entire scheme the minute the gossip about Kathleen's new job reached him. He had been blackballed at home and winning Connor's confidence through his association with Kathleen had been his last desperate hope.

If only she hadn't fallen for Brian's sad story when he first came to Shea Crystal. He had been so believable. How could she not give him a chance to pay back all the people he owed? She couldn't turn her back on someone who needed help. Now she understood why Brian was capable of misleading clients so easily. It wasn't that they were naive, it was that he was so expert at presenting a facade of sincerity. She had set aside her own previous doubts and accepted him at face value.

When Connor returned from Limerick, she would apprise him of the latest turn in Brian's plans. When he found out that Brian was investing Shea Crystal's money in some high-flying schemes, he would back out of their business alliance and demand his money back. She only hoped there was money left to return.

The next morning, Kathleen plunged into writing copy for the catalog. She skipped lunch and pushed herself until past dinner. Theresa tried to reason with her that she was working too hard, but Kathleen was determined to get ahead of schedule. Then she could take time out and put some space between herself and Land's End. She needed to think things through without distractions. And Brian was definitely a distraction.

She told Theresa she wanted to spend some time visiting her parents' hometown. The time off wouldn't interfere with her deadline on the catalog. She had very little left to do.

Theresa was surprised at the sudden decision. "Don't you want to wait until Connor returns from Limerick? I know he would be happy to accompany you on this trip."

"It's something best done alone," Kathleen said. "Besides, he would probably be bored." She did not want to burden Theresa with her true reason for not waiting for Connor.

"Is there a problem between you and Connor? Is that why he didn't come back with you?"

"I don't know what happened, Theresa. Connor had business in Limerick, but he didn't want to discuss it with me, and he left rather abruptly."

"I thought things were going well . . . that you

and Connor . . . Kathleen, whatever it is, wouldn't it be better to wait for Connor to return so you can try and work it out? You've become my dearest friend. I'll do anything I can to help."

"Don't worry about me, Theresa. I simply need some time alone. Just a couple of days. Can you arrange it for me? I'd like to rent a car and visit Crossmolina, and maybe spend a night in Westport, too."

"Of course. I have a friend in Westport who has a bed and breakfast. You will be comfortable there. She may be able to arrange a car, too."

Kathleen packed an overnight bag and Theresa drove her to Westport. They embraced before parting and Kathleen wasn't sure if the tear that dampened her cheek was her own or Connor's sister's.

The accommodations at the Westport farmhouse, perched on a rise overlooking Clew Bay, were cozy and the proprietress fussed about, giving Kathleen special attention. It amused Kathleen; Theresa must have told her hostess a bit about the situation.

After dinner, Kathleen went for a walk. She took a path through a cow pasture with the resident collie at her side. The air was damp and chill but the day was clear and the bay water glistened. Hawks screeched as they launched into flight in search of their last meal of the day.

Kathleen ruffled the collie's neck fur and the dog nuzzled her hand. Sadness enveloped her. She would miss Ireland. The people she had met were warm and friendly, accepting her immediately. She knew that the acceptance was partly due to her association with Connor, but it went beyond that. They were generous people, ready to offer a stranger a cup of tea and a few minutes' conversation any time.

She had even considered Theresa's suggestion that she remain at Shea Crystal and head up the projected in-house advertising campaign. That was out of the question now. Too many misunderstandings. And if Brian cheated Connor, which was a definite possibility, it might cast doubt on her own character.

The collie suddenly ran ahead and disappeared over a rise. Kathleen could hear him barking at her to follow. She jogged over the crest of the hill. The dog had evidently chased a chipmunk or squirrel into a deserted thatched-roof cottage. A rock wall abutted the old building. She sat on it a moment and called to the collie. It stubbornly scratched at the door, trying to pry it open far enough to squeeze through.

Kathleen walked over to the dog and tugged its collar. She peered inside the dilapidated building. The shutters on the opposite wall gaped open. Sunlight streamed across the dirt floor. A family with simple needs had once lived here. Simple needs and little stress. What a gift. She would gladly exchange her computer and car for the ease of daily chores that tied you to the earth. She could visualize the woman who once lived here milking cows and walking the peaceful hills in the sunlight.

But her daydreams did not imitate reality. No one's life was totally void of hard times. Exchanging one set of problems for another accomplished nothing. There had been famine in Ireland, and every family faced illness, sadness and death along with the pleasant times.

Her relationship with Connor had had pleasant times, too, and to think that it would all be smooth sailing was foolish. He was moody and she had to accept that facet of his personality.

She was thankful that she had told him her misgivings about Brian. Not that she had suggested that Brian had been underhanded at Harris and Forbes, but at least she had told him of the rumors. Which was all she knew. If she hadn't leveled with him early on, she would have painted herself into a corner.

The collie danced around her feet, ready for a new adventure. Kathleen turned and they made their way back to the guest house.

That night, Kathleen tossed to dreams filled with scenes of Connor. He was standing on a hill with his arms open, calling her name. She ran to meet him, but when she reached the crest of the hill, he was gone. Variations of the scene caused a restless sleep.

Waking before daylight, she dressed quickly and slipped outside. She hiked along the deserted roadside, her step quick. At sunrise, she found herself at the base of Croagh Patrick. Quite a few people were beginning the trek up the hill. Kathleen climbed to the plateau where St. Patrick's statue guarded the mountain. A young nun, brown oxfords hanging around her neck by the laces, nodded her head in greeting.

The terrain was rugged, covered with sharp lava-like cinder. Kathleen's gaze traveled up the steep mountainside and the switch-back trail. It was like watching an evacuation in a war movie. Everyone marched slowly and persistently, casting aside discomfort in their zealous devotion to their patron saint.

"St. Patrick, you may think you drove all the snakes out of Ireland, but you missed a modern-day viper, one of the worst," Kathleen said under her breath.

She climbed higher, working off her anger toward Brian.

On either side of her, the Irish struggled up the hill. An elderly woman, gnarled and tired looking, leaned on a younger duplication of herself. A farmer wearing heavy work boots stopped to remove them before joining the processional.

They were a determined lot, and Kathleen was of the same stock. Her mother had made this pilgrimage undaunted and so would she.

At the pinnacle of the mountain Kathleen rested with the others. Her feet were sore, her calves cramped. But the exhaustion and pain were laced with the satisfaction of reaching a goal shared with her parents' countrymen. They treated her as one of their own, smiling, sharing a jug of brook water, never doubting that she belonged. Perhaps they were right.

It was noon when Kathleen returned to the farmhouse. Her hostess had arranged a car rental and had outlined the road to Crossmolina on a map.

Soon a wooden signpost indicated that she was nearing her parents' town. The farmland was verdant and cottages dotted the roadside. Kathleen's heart began to race and familiarity washed over her. She could almost see her mother's face, hear her mother's voice. Crossmolina had been the focal point for all the bedtimes stories her mother had regaled her with as a child.

Kathleen slowed the car as she entered Crossmolina, then parked. It seemed strange walking along the very street her parents had walked before she was born. She stopped to look into the windows of the chemist's shop. Veterinary supplies were displayed side by side with rubbing liniment and Swiss watches. The mercantile store had bolts of bright plaid woolens standing tall in the window; the tea shop was filled with lunch patrons enjoying tea and scones.

The constabulary, where her mother was born, was now the Dolphin Inn. She stepped inside and ordered a cold glass of mineral water and spoke to the barmaid. The woman remembered Kathleen's family and was delighted to pass time with her, sharing reminiscences.

Kathleen felt as though her mother were holding her hand, walking the streets of the quaint Irish town with her.

Next, Kathleen drove to Gortner Abbey. It was an impressive campus, reminiscent of eastern finishing schools.

She remembered her mother confiding that as a non-Catholic she often felt out of place at the convent school. When nagging insecurities plagued her, she and a favorite nun would take a boat out on the bay and talk. The fishing excursions not only provided the cook with a rucksack of fish, but thanks to the empathetic nun, it gave her mother a newly restored self-image. Her mother credited the nun with infusing her with the courage to marry outside of her own faith.

Kathleen left the school and drove to the churchyard, her final stop. She nosed the car against the rock fence and got out. A breeze ruffled her hair and she brushed the errant strands from her face.

She was surprised by a tear that dampened her finger. She hadn't realized that she was crying.

The cemetery was small, many of the graves unattended. Yet they didn't look neglected. There was something touching in the natural growth of buttercups and shamrocks that tumbled about the stones.

Kathleen stepped across and around grave markers until she found her mother's family's plot. Her grandparents' names were etched into a large granite stone. She looked just beyond and instinctively knew that her father's people were only steps away.

She hadn't thought to bring flowers, but wildflowers cascaded from the rock wall. She yanked a handful of the golden blossoms from a crevice and solemnly placed them on the sod. The flowers rested against the stone. Kathleen pressed her fingertips into the grooves that spelled out her grandparents' epitaph.

Tears spilled from her eyes, but they were not borne of sadness. She was glad she had come. It was as though her life had been a book with a page torn out. Tracing her beginnings made the story whole.

As she walked through the churchyard, she thought ruefully that her past might now be whole but her future was incomplete.

She would return to Shea Crystal in the morning to finish the catalog. She would also confront Connor and determine where their relationship stood.

They had to talk. And if things did not work out, she would put aside her dream of being part of his life. She would return to San Francisco and try to pick up the pieces of her shattered life. The sooner that was accomplished, the better.

Chapter Fifteen

Brian was gone when Kathleen returned to Land's End. She was relieved that one barrier to concentration had been removed, and she could set her mind on finishing the catalog.

Theresa and Sean had set their wedding date and Theresa insisted that Kathleen be her maid of honor. Although Kathleen argued that she did not expect to remain in Ireland long enough, Theresa won out and she agreed to stay.

Kathleen and Theresa spent a weekend in Galway looking for a wedding dress for Theresa and an appropriate gown for Kathleen. Theresa fell in love with a white satin tea-length dress with illusion lace sleeves and neckline. She chose a short veil with a headpiece of satin rosebuds.

While it was love at first sight for Theresa, Kathleen's dress hunt was not so easy. Every garment she tried on seemed unsuitable. Color was wrong, style was too young, cut was too revealing or it did not fit. Finally, Theresa sat her down in the dressing room of a fine boutique and told Kathleen that every dress she had tried on had looked good on her. She simply was resisting being in the wedding party.

Kathleen tried to deny that, but knew that Theresa was right. She finally settled on a Victorian-style peach satin and lace dress. Too romantic, she thought, but it made Theresa happy.

In between appointments for fittings they lunched at a quaint restaurant on the waterfront. The bay that once epitomized Kathleen's image of this gentle land seemed as flat as her spirits.

The reception would be held at Land's End and Jennie was in her glory planning the details. An arbor had been constructed and whitewashed. Kathleen was shown a sketch of what it would look like with white lilies, baby's breath and ivy entwined around the arch. Connor was not sparing cost; the flowers were being flown in from a hothouse in England.

Instead of being contagious, Theresa's ebullience about her forthcoming marriage depressed Kathleen. The bride-to-be's prenuptial radiance accented Kathleen's loss.

She had not been able to speak to Connor since

he returned from Limerick. He was constantly on the go with appointments away from the office. His meals were on the run. He was working double-time, his energies immersed in the high-priority projects that the catalog and the cooperative presented.

Somehow she had to catch him, talk to him, find out what was wrong. If they didn't clear the air soon, Theresa's wedding, the high point of *her* life, would be the low point of Kathleen's.

How could she stand beside Connor and not miss the warmth that she once thought might be hers forever? It would be devastating to have emotional distance between them, when they were physically linked by circumstance.

Would she have to dance with him at the reception? How could she melt into the strength of Connor's arms without his being aware of her love? Could he ignore the closeness that they once shared? Would a spark of remembrance ignite a renewed desire between them? And if it did, would either one of them dare act upon that desire? Questions, so many questions, and no answers.

Each evening, after dinner, Kathleen worked on the cooperative catalog, determined that Theresa would not have to shoulder that burden.

True to her word, she shopped a catalog for computer equipment and software to initiate the company into the technological age. Theresa had not restricted her to a budget, but Kathleen carefully conserved their money, looking for bargains along with quality.

She had given Clare and Theresa a few lessons on her Powerbook. Surprisingly, Clare did not balk at the proposed change in office procedure. Kathleen had expected opposition, but Clare confided that it was about time Shea Crystal "got with it." Her sister in Cork had been using a computer for six years and Clare had felt left behind with notepad and pen as her main tools. She couldn't wait to tell her sister the good news.

All through the morning, Connor's associates paraded through her office to drop off photographs of their products and to offer suggestions. Sincere affection had developed between them. They often dawdled, and Kathleen sensed that when she left Ireland she would be missed.

Kathleen knew that Connor was scheduled to remain in his office most of the day. Theresa had told her that Sean planned to meet with him at noon, and a representative from the cooperative had set up a meeting for three o'clock.

She finished proofing the catalog galleys at two o'clock, and headed for Connor's office. It was a first-rate catalog and her name would appear on the credit page. This project would be her ticket for reentry into advertising any place she elected to settle. She tried to push out of her mind the thought that she wanted to settle here, in Ireland.

Meeting her goals gave her confidence; now was the time to confront Connor.

Kathleen knocked on Connor's office door, then entered. Connor was standing, looking out the window. He turned to face her. As always, her heart leaped at the sight of him.

"I've proofed the galleys; they're ready to go to press." She placed the roll of papers on his desk.

"You finished with time to spare, Kathleen." He scanned the papers. "You've done a good job. More than good; it's a fine job."

Kathleen knew this was her chance. While the achievement of completing the catalog kept her adrenaline pumping, she would demand to know what was wrong between them.

"We need to talk. When you ran off to Limerick without letting me know what was going on, I didn't know what to think. You treated me badly, Connor. And you've avoided me since you returned."

"The telegram I received in Dublin was disturbing. It was about my Connemara sketch. There was the possibility that it had been offered to a competing glassworks by an intermediary. The manager thought he recognized my initials. It wasn't a certainty, and I had to go and identify it."

"Why didn't you tell me?"

"I wasn't ready to discuss it. What if it wasn't my sketch? Why should both of us be disappointed?

"It turned out Brian's signature was on the sales

contract. The glassworks immediately stopped payment on the check when I confirmed that the design was mine. I was angry that I had been duped. Angry at Brian and angry at myself for being taken in. I didn't want to discuss it, I just wanted to concentrate on work and put it behind me."

"Brian stole your sketches?"

"Yes. He evidently wasn't satisfied with earning a commission by representing Shea Crystal, he planned to make a profit by hijacking my design."

"On the way home from Dublin Brian bragged about investing clients' money while waiting for contracts to come through. I told him that was underhanded and I realized he couldn't be trusted. But stealing! I never would have suspected him to go that far."

"Greed can be a strong motivator for someone who is low on ethics. I was glad that you told me about the rumors. It made it easier to believe that Brian was the culprit. After all, he is a pretty likable fellow."

"Yes," Kathleen said. "And he traded on his charm. He fooled people who thought they knew him quite well, including me. I'm sorry he caused so much trouble."

"I consider Brian a bad investment, nothing more. Shea Crystal can afford the loss. It's going to be a good year. Last night we were notified that our design won the Connemara competition. We'll be gearing up for double production. That means more jobs, lass."

"Connor, that's wonderful."

Kathleen had some unfinished business. "But Connor, you should have told me about the telegram, about Brian's duplicity. Not being open can destroy a relationship. Do you have any idea what this misunderstanding caused? I thought that you were avoiding me, and I had no idea why. I was devastated."

"I didn't mean to upset you. When I returned from Limerick there was so much to do, so many deadlines to meet. I was constantly running out of time. It seemed whenever I was here, you were there. Responsibilities kept piling up.

"I wanted to be with you. I never thought you would question my love."

"Love?" She had conjured dreams of his declaring his love, but never expected it to be uttered so matter-of-factly.

How like him to have assumed that she knew he loved her, that his actions spoke the words he had not verbalized.

"How could I know your feelings, Connor? Love is an awesome concept. You never spoke about love. I thought that what we shared might have been nothing more than a romantic attraction."

He pulled her close until she was tightly tucked into the circle of his arms. "I love you, Kathleen."

"I love you too, Connor, with all my heart. But you have to be open; you have to talk about what's important to you, to us. Don't keep me in the dark."

"I'm sorry, Kathleen, I should have spoken sooner. About many things, but especially about my feelings for you."

He touched the side of her face, tilting it to meet his, and his mouth captured hers. The kiss was a promise of things to come. She would not leave Ireland, she would forever be a part of this land.

"Shall we plan a double wedding?" Connor asked. "Theresa would be delighted."

Marriage. She hadn't allowed herself to think that far ahead. To know that Connor loved her was all she desired at the moment. Marriage was icing on the cake and almost too sweet to comprehend. Yet she knew that deep in her heart it was the way she had prayed their relationship would end. But it wasn't an ending, it was a new beginning.

"I know that it's a big decision to leave your homeland, but with Shea's entry into the American trade we'll be going back and forth often."

Kathleen pressed her fingers to his lips. "Shush. You don't have to promise anything to persuade me, Connor. As long as we're together, I'll be content."

And that was true. Kathleen's home would be with Connor, wherever that might be.

"We must tell Theresa," Connor said.

"Yes, but first there's something far more urgent to attend to."

She pulled his face to hers and initiated a kiss that left no doubt as to the depth of her love.

Kathleen was home at last . . . in her lover's arms, in the emerald land that claimed her as its own.